Something is preventing Julie Covington from making a decision.

Two hours later the quiz was over and Julie was relieved. Not one of her shining efforts. But then, she was only in the class because she needed the general credits for graduation. Maybe if she were more interested in sociology she would not have had such a problem studying. Leaving the classroom with a sigh, Julie turned her face to the autumn sun and felt the soft breeze ripple her blond hair. The day was a gentle one, warm but without the intensity of the summer's heat, and refreshing without bordering on blustery. Even the light seemed softer than a few weeks ago, less intense, more fluid.

Julie decided she had enough time to head back to her dorm to freshen up before meeting Dennis for supper. They had been going along comfortably enough as two students at the same school. Now, with the job offer pending, there would be a wedge building between them until they decided something about the future. More accurately, it was up to her to decide something about the future. Dennis had made his intentions clear over and over again. Julie was the one who couldn't commit herself.

SUSANNAH HAYDEN is the pen name of a versatile and gifted author of fiction and biography for both adults and children. Susannah makes her home in Illinois with her husband and children.

Books by Susannah Hayden

HEARTSONG PRESENTS
HP14—A Matter of Choice
HP69—Between Love and Loyalty
HP77—The Road Before Me
HP113—Between the Memory and the Moment

ROMANCE READER—TWO BOOKS IN ONE
RR9—Summer's Wind Blowing & Spring Waters Rushing

Don't miss out on any of our super romances. Write to us at the following address for information on our newest releases and club information.

Heartsong Presents Readers' Service
P.O. Box 719
Uhrichsville, OH 44683

Farther
Along the Road

Susannah Hayden

A sequel to *The Road Before Me.*

Heartsong Presents

A note from the Author:

I love to hear from my readers! You may write to me at the following address:

Susannah Hayden
Author Relations
P.O. Box 719
Uhrichsville, OH 44683

ISBN 1-55748-687-5

FARTHER ALONG THE ROAD

one

Light streaked through the smudged window and dust swirled delicately in the air when Julie Covington pulled on the cord and parted the drooping beige draperies. For a moment, she watched the particles dance on the sunbeam before holding her breath and waving away the dust with a grimace. She turned away from the window to inspect the dorm room, flipping her blond hair over her shoulder as she did.

It was the same dormitory she had lived in the previous year and all the rooms were alike: two twin beds, two desks, and one bookcase. Two sets of drawers were built into the wall between two closets that had folding fan doors. Julie's roommate, Melanie, would arrive on Sunday, so for now she had the room to herself. After the recent chaos and commotion at her family's home, she was glad to be alone for two days as she contemplated her last year of college.

Julie's summer had been a strange one. Against the advice of her parents she had loaded up her compact station wagon, left Illinois, and headed to Seabridge, Maine to spend the summer painting. At least that was the excuse she gave for leaving her family—and Dennis—for ten weeks. The truth was a bit more complicated.

She brushed her bangs out of her blue eyes. Rummaging through a cardboard box perched on the bare mattress of the bed she had claimed, Julie pulled out a sketch pad and flipped through its pages. She had made drawing after drawing of Leed House, the enormous old New England home in which her grandmother had grown up. After years of neglect and vacancy, Leed House was being converted into a bed and breakfast inn that would once again know voices echoing in the hallways and the vitality of lives passing through its rooms. The grandeur of the pre-Depression era would be captured for a new generation.

Although her grandmother had told her many stories about Leed House, Julie had never seen it until last summer. What she thought would be a one-day stop to find the old house had turned into a ten-week stay in Seabridge. Once they discovered who she was, the owners insisted that she come as often as she wanted to sketch and paint on the property.

Della Paxton was a fiftyish, energetic, graying widow who talked incessantly and refused to take no for an answer. Julie had liked her instantly. Her son, Larry, was a twenty-eight year-old accountant who had given up the fast track and donned a carpenter's belt to help his mother with the vast remodeling project. In contrast to his mother, Larry hardly talked at all. For the most part, he minded his own business. It had been hard to get to know Larry; Julie found him as mysterious as his mother was engaging. Unfortunately she had embarrassed herself by allowing feelings to develop that Larry did not return. She had done the sensible thing and had come home to Dennis. But the dark, mysterious presence of Larry Paxton lingered in her mind.

Julie reached into her shirt pocket and pulled out the note she had received from Della only yesterday.

> *Dear Julie,*
>   *This old place is so lonely without you. We both got rather accustomed to having you around. When will we see you again?*
>   *Thank you so much for leaving the painting of the front view of the house. You worked so hard on it. We*

are honored to have it, and it will have a place of prominence, I assure you. Larry has decided to make a frame for it himself. That tells you something of what he thinks of it. Do stay in touch and let us know when you can visit again.

Fondly,
Della

She would like to go back to Leed House, Julie was sure of that. But her future was up for grabs. First she had to finish college. Then there was the question of getting a job. Had majoring in art been very practical? And of course there was Dennis. He had tried as hard as he could to understand her need to be away for the summer. And despite her waffling emotions, his love for her never wavered. She knew that soon she would have to decide whether her future was with Dennis.

Julie's musings were interrupted by the arrival of her oldest sister, Marjorie, precariously balancing an armload of clothes on hangers.

"You sure you want all this stuff here?" Marjorie asked. "Your closet is not very big."

"It's big enough." Julie stepped across the room and took some of the clothes from Marjorie's load. She started hanging them in the closet.

"You really won't need your winter things for a couple of months," Marjorie persisted. "Why don't you leave them at home for a while?"

"I want them here," Julie said simply. She had long ago given up defending her choices to her sister. With a fifteen-year difference in their ages, Marjorie had always tried to run Julie's life. Nothing Julie decided ever satisfied Marjorie. She meant well, Julie knew, but this was one relationship that

Julie had not missed while she was away for the summer.

"Well, I guess we'd better get another load," Julie said, and started for the door.

Marjorie followed. "Those stairs are killers. You're a senior. Couldn't you have gotten a room on the first floor this year?'

"I like the light better on the third floor," Julie answered matter-of-factly.

A few minutes later they were huffing up the stairs with boxes of art supplies. Julie fully expected Marjorie to launch into her usual speech about how it was not practical to major in art. Julie had heard it a hundred times—there's no money in being an artist. The odds of being successful are low. Sketching is not a marketable skill. How would she be able to support herself? Artists are not in touch with reality.

Even if all those things were true, Julie could not help herself. She had to draw; she had to paint; she had to be able to see the dust dancing on the sunbeam. What Marjorie, and nearly everyone else, never understood was that Julie did not make a conscious choice to be an artist. She simply was one.

But Marjorie was not remarking on Julie's artistic bent today. For a change, she just carried the box of paints and pads to the the third floor and set it in the corner.

"Maybe we should start emptying some of these boxes," Marjorie said with her usual practicality. "I can flatten them and take them back to my house."

"Sure," Julie said, reaching for a box of books. Methodically she filled the top shelf of the bookcase, while Marjorie unpacked her computer and got it set up on the desk.

"I think Grammy really missed you while you were gone," Marjorie said as she ducked her head behind the desk in search of an outlet.

Julie looked up, a little startled. "Do you really think so?

She hasn't really responded to me since I came home."

"She seemed more frustrated than usual," Marjorie said, "almost depressed."

Julie's shoulders sagged and she sighed heavily. "I missed her, too. But I've been missing her for a long time."

Marjorie nodded. "I know. It's been hard to watch the Alzheimer's make her so—"

"Gone," Julie said flatly. "She's just not there." She straightened her row of books for the third time. "How's Daddy doing? He hasn't really talked to me."

Marjorie shrugged. "Things haven't changed much. Aunt Jane and Aunt Fran are still on the rampage, insisting that Dad do something about Grammy."

Irritation rose up in Julie. "What do they want him to do? He's already taken Grammy into his home. . .something neither of them were willing to do."

"They really don't have space, Julie. You know that."

"Yes, I know. How convenient." Her tone had turned sarcastic. "Even if they lived in mansions, they would still expect Daddy to 'do something about the problem.'"

"Well," Marjorie said grudgingly, "I hate to admit it, but you may be right about that."

"I know I am." Julie was adamant. She shoved another book in the bookcase.

"Take it easy, Julie."

"I can't help it. Jane and Fran are Grammy's daughters, but they just treat her like a problem they wish would go away. Daddy is just trying to keep peace in the family. But he's busy, so Mom gets stuck with all the work. No one helps. It's obviously wearing her out."

Marjorie was quiet. "Jane and Fran are pushing for a nursing home." Julie groaned, but Marjorie jumped back in before she could protest. "I know you don't like that; everyone knows you don't like it. But it's reality. Mom can't handle Grammy much longer. . .no one can. She's getting dangerous."

Julie looked up sharply. "Has she hurt someone again?"

"I thought you knew."

"No one said anything."

"She almost dislocated Mom's elbow. She was having a fit while Mom was trying to give her a bath. She pinned Mom against the wall and twisted her arm."

"Oh no," Julie gasped.

"Dad got home just in time."

"Why didn't anyone tell me?" Julie demanded.

"We all know how you feel about Grammy."

"But I don't want Mom to get hurt."

"Nobody does. That's why we think a nursing home is a good idea."

A tear slipped out of one eye. Julie quickly wiped it away.

Marjorie pushed the power button on the computer to make sure it was working. "You're all set. I'll take these empty boxes back to the van and get another load."

Julie nodded. "I'll be down in a minute." She swallowed the lump in her throat. Grammy in an impersonal, sterile nursing home. . .she hated to even think about that possibility. But it was becoming a reality. Grammy could be difficult to handle physically. The Alzheimer's had taken away her mind but left her physical strength. It was as if all her former mental energy was now channeled physically and she could easily overpower someone caring for her.

Reluctantly, Julie started down the stairs, dragging an empty box behind her. On the landing of the second floor, she nearly ran into Dennis.

"Julie? Are you all right?" he asked.

She looked into his eyes, unable to form any words. Gently

he took the box from her hand and waited for a response.

"I'm okay," she finally said. She offered her lips for a quick kiss and Dennis obliged. "I've just been talking with Marjorie about Grammy. It's the same old story. I just hate to watch what's happening."

Dennis took her into his arms and held her close, without speaking.

"Knock it off, you two." Marjorie was on her way back up the stairs. "There's work to do."

Dennis stepped away from Julie and grinned at Marjorie.

"There are only three boxes left," Marjorie said. "Why don't you grab those and help Julie finish unpacking. I need to get going pretty soon."

"Be right up." Dennis scrambled down the stairs. Julie and Marjorie went back up to the third floor to wait for Dennis.

"Tell Mom I'll be home tomorrow night for the weekend," Julie said.

Marjorie nodded. "With everything that's happening in the family, it's a good thing school is close to home."

"I'm going to try to see Grammy every weekend."

"Don't let your studies suffer," Marjorie warned.

"I can handle it."

Dennis entered the room with three boxes stacked in his arms.

"Oh, great, you're back," Marjorie said. "I gotta get going. The girls will be out of school soon."

Julie leaned over and kissed her sister's cheek perfunctorily. "Thanks for all your help."

"No problem. See you on the weekend."

Marjorie left and Julie turned to give Dennis a weak smile.

"You're worn out, aren't you?" Dennis said.

She nodded. "I've been back home for only two weeks, but all the pressure is already getting to me."

"Have I told you how glad I am that you're back?"

"Only about twelve times a day."

"And I mean it every time." He held his hand out and she took it.

She wanted to change the focus of their conversation. "By Christmas, you'll be done with this place."

Dennis smiled. He was ready to enter the work world and was confident about it, unlike Julie.

"You won't be far behind me," he said. "We're on the verge of a whole new era."

She smiled, but falsely. She was not at all sure she was ready for a whole new era.

two

"Hey, look what the cat dragged in." Ted Covington lathered mayonnaise generously on a slice of bread as his baby sister came through the back door on Friday afternoon.

"What are you doing here?" Julie put her book bag on the counter, pinched her brother's bread, and popped the morsel in her mouth.

"Mom was lonely for me," Ted said. "She begged me to come for dinner tonight."

"Right," Julie said skeptically. "That's why you're feeding your face with that hideous sandwich."

"Oh, this," Ted said, adding a thick slice of ham and some ketchup. "Just an appetizer. Dinner is not for hours. Marjorie's coming, too."

Julie rolled her eyes. "And the kids, I suppose. It's going to be chaos around here. Let's go to your place."

Ted, his mouth full, said, "No can do. That would go against my code of honor."

Julie hoisted herself up to sit on the counter and leaned her head back against a cabinet. She studied her attorney brother. "Since when did you get so noble? You've been known to duck out of a family problem before. I've always admired your ability to avoid confrontation."

"Don't flatter me." Ted took a huge bite of his concoction, but kept talking. "I'm a middle child. I had to learn certain skills just to survive four sisters."

"Lisa and Terry did the smart thing." Julie was thinking of her two sisters who lived out of state.

"Moving away?" Ted raised his eyebrows.

Julie nodded.

Ted shrugged. "Lisa was offered a great job in Denver. How could she not go?"

"I know, I know," Julie mumbled. "And Terry moved to Sacramento because Rick got transferred. Perfectly legitimate reasons. Still, it doesn't seem fair that they don't have to deal with all the mess around here."

Ted met his youngest sister's blue eyes. "May I respectfully remind you that you left, too?"

"But I came back. And I'm going to come home from school every weekend."

Ted chewed thoughtfully, a brown curl dangling on his forehead.

"Let's talk about something else."

Julie hopped down from the counter and crossed the room to the refrigerator.

"Okay. How's that loverboy of yours?" He took another enormous bite.

Julie grimaced as she reached for an apple. "Why do you insist on calling him that?"

"To see the expression on your face. But I'll rephrase my question if you'd like."

"Please do."

Ted furrowed his brow and looked sternly at Julie. "Miss Covington, just what are the intentions of that young man of yours?"

"Oh, that is so much better." She picked up a dish towel and absently started polishing her apple. "I assure you, his intentions are most honorable."

"So when are you going to announce your engagement?"

Julie bit her apple and replied casually, "Who said anything about getting engaged?"

"Everything sure points that way."

"Well, don't put the cart before the horse."

Ted stopped chewing and looked at her sternly. "Are you toying with that boy's affections?"

Julie sank into a chair next to her brother and brushed her blond hair away from her face. Ted had always been the only sibling she could really talk to. How much should she tell him now?

"Dennis puts up with a lot from me. He's far too patient."

"You're faulting the guy for being patient with you?"

Julie shrugged. "Sounds pretty stupid, huh?"

"What do you want from him?"

"I guess that's the problem. I can't point to one specific thing, one trait that I wish were different. But somehow, something's not right."

"He's a great guy and he's crazy about you. What's wrong with that?"

"We spend so much time together. Sometimes I feel like I'm just an extension of Dennis. I don't know if I want to marry someone like that."

Ted sighed and muttered, "Women."

"Don't start on that tirade," Julie warned.

The back door opened and Marjorie entered, followed reluctantly by her two elementary school-age daughters. Without acknowledging Ted or Julie, the girls sauntered through the kitchen to the family room and turned on the television.

"Another heartwarming family moment," Ted said dryly, watching the little girls stretch out on the floor, their faces propped in their hands, too close to the television.

"Knock it off," Marjorie said. "It's already been a long day." Her heels clicked against the tile floor as she crossed the room. She opened the refrigerator and pushed things around to make space for the salad she had brought with her. "Where's Mom?"

"Upstairs," Ted said, "with Grammy."

"Why are you two sitting here pigging out?" Marjorie reprimanded. "She could probably use some help getting dinner going."

Julie and Ted looked at each other sheepishly. Ted reluctantly put down his sandwich.

All three of them jumped when they heard the crash at the top of the stairs. Marjorie was the first to hurtle up the stairs; Julie and Ted scrambled close behind.

In the upstairs hall they found Grammy sitting on top of their mother. Her face was red and she moaned incoherently. The floor was strewn with shards of glass, the fragments of a broken photo frame. Their parents' wedding photo had an ugly scratch across the center of it.

"Get her off of me!" Liz cried. "Be careful of the glass." Vainly she tried to writhe away from her mother-in-law.

After a moment of shock the siblings sprang into action. Ted firmly placed his arms under his grandmother's armpits and began to lift. She resisted his efforts and flailed her arms more ferociously. Finding his chest she pummeled her fists against him. Ted ducked to get his face out of the way. Julie and Marjorie grabbed for their grandmother's arms, finally succeeding at restraining her.

It took all three of them to calm her down and move her down the hall to her room. Finally free, Liz sat up to catch her breath.

"What happened here?" boomed a bass voice.

Julie looked over her shoulder to see her father picking up glass and staring at his wife. Liz Covington fell gratefully against her husband, Tom, as he knelt next to her. He wrapped his arms around her and looked anxiously down the hall at his three grown children trying to control one elderly woman.

Julie met her father's eyes for a moment and saw the searing pain they held. It cut right through her. She wanted to go to her parents but was afraid to let go of her grip on her grandmother.

They wrestled Grammy into her room and made her sit in the armchair that had been her favorite for thirty years. Experience had taught them that that particular chair with its worn upholstery and bad springs usually helped to settle her down.

"This has got to stop," Marjorie said adamantly, releasing her hold. "When is somebody going to do something about it?"

"Shhh," Ted hushed his sister. "Don't do that here," he whispered harshly.

Marjorie took a deep breath and got control of her fury. "You two will have to handle this. I'm going to go see how Mom is." She left without looking at her grandmother again.

Ted and Julie looked at each other without speaking. Julie stroked Grammy's hand while Ted tucked an afghan around her, both of them making an effort to make her feel secure.

Grammy was calmer now.

"I'll stay with her," Julie said. "Go find out if Mom is okay."

"Are you sure?"

"She seems fine now. She doesn't usually have two episodes close together. I'll be all right."

Ted still looked doubtful.

"Go, please," Julie insisted. "I'll be fine."

Ted leaned down and kissed his grandmother's blank face before leaving. Julie listened to his footsteps as he went back downstairs; she did not envy the conversation he would join in another moment. Part of her reason for offering to stay with Grammy was selfish. She did not want to be part of the discussion about what to do with Grammy.

As Julie predicted, it was only minutes before the voices in the kitchen rose to the level that she could hear them upstairs. Their words were muffled, but the tone of the discussion was clear. Her father's bass voice, which he hardly ever raised, resonated against the ceiling. Her mother was talking in clipped tones that betrayed her fear. Marjorie was trying to be reasonable and Ted was being sympathetic to all sides.

She knew what they must be saying. And it was true. They could not take care of Grammy anymore. Even Julie had to admit that the time had come to seek real help.

She stroked Grammy's hand in a steady rhythm. The old woman began to mutter, almost imperceptibly.

"Grammy?" Julie stooped in front of her grandmother's chair, vainly searching for any sign of recognition. "Grammy, it's me, Julie. Do you need something?"

Grammy's head twitched from side to side. Her eyes did not focus. She struggled to form words. "Co. . .co. . .where co. . .?"

"Oh, Grammy, where have you gone?"

Julie settled onto the arm of the chair with a hand on her grandmother's shoulder. Her thoughts went to a green leather book she had read during her summer in Maine.

In the midst of his remodeling work, Larry Paxton had discovered an old diary in the wall that divided the two parlors of Leed House. Apparently the wall was not original to the house, and when it was erected, the diary had been trapped inside it. The book told the story of a young woman's first love. Her heart had beat for a handsome, bearded Italian man of whom her family did not approve. Julie had followed the ill-fated story to the end, only to discover that the writer had been her own grandmother.

Grammy had been denied her first love and no one in the family had ever known about it. Even now, Julie had not told anyone in her family about the diary she had discovered or the secrets it contained. She longed to hear more of the story from her grandmother, Julienne Leed Covington, for whom she had been named. She wished that somehow she could communicate to Grammy that she knew about the pain of her youth. And, most of all, she wanted to know if Grammy had loved Colin Covington when she married him or if she had finally succumbed to her family's pressure to make a suitable marriage. Had she ever gotten over Lorenzo Scorzo?

Julie would most likely never know the answers to these questions. During her ten-week summer absence, Grammy's blank eyes had become even more vacant. Julie had not thought that possible, but it had happened. She had come home to find the old woman even more out of reach. Grammy was not passive—far from it. A fire burned within her, its flames leaping and dancing. But their heat served only to sear closed any access to the outside world. Sometimes she would utter syllables that were recognizable, even words or whole phrases. But it was hard to know what she was talking about without more context that she could give. Although Grammy would sometimes babble continuously for twenty minutes, no one could understand what she said. And no one could explain the sudden violent eruptions of her emotions.

Grammy's eyes were closed, though she still sat upright in the chair.

Julie got off of her perch and gently took her grandmother's hand. "Grammy, would you like to lie down for a little while?"

In stark contrast to her behavior of an hour ago, Grammy compliantly let her namesake lead her to the bed and tuck the sheet around her. She was asleep almost immediately. Looking at the peaceful picture before her now, it was difficult for Julie to believe that this thin, ninety-two-year-old woman was capable of what they had all witnessed in the hall earlier.

But the vision of Grammy, sitting on top of her mother, was still fresh in Julie's mind.

With one last kiss on her grandmother's sleeping face, Julie left the room and went to join the family downstairs.

three

Julie woke early the next morning. The house was still, with no evidence of the rising emotions of the night before. After a tense dinner, Marjorie and Ted had gone back to their homes. Julie had made a pot of tea and sat with her mother, neither of them saying much. Finally, they had gone to bed.

But Julie had not slept well. Her dreams were invaded by gruesome images of faces distorted and swollen, eyes gleaming strangely, mouths open but silent. Some she almost recognized, but then they would stretch and twist and slither away, fading into blackness. Other faces were unknown to her, but she studied them in her dream, frantically searching for something she recognized. What did it all mean? Twice during the night Julie got up for a glass of water, but both times the dreams returned, haunting her sleep all night.

She was relieved when morning came, its light chasing away her tormenters. She padded down the hall to the bathroom and splashed some cold water on her face. A shower could wait. For now, she just ran a comb through her hair and tied her summer robe securely at the waist.

Next she went to Grammy's room. Her grandmother had woken briefly during the evening and Julie had coaxed her into eating something. But the old woman had soon gone back to bed for the night, looking as harmless as a sleeping infant.

Julie turned the knob of her grandmother's door as slowly as she could to avoid the usual click. She opened the door just wide enough to enter and went and sat in the armchair. For a few moments, she simply watched Grammy's rhythmic breathing. Softly, Grammy began to stir.

"Co. . .train. . .home. . .no, no."

Julie moved to the bed and sat next to her grandmother. "Grammy? Are you awake?"

The old woman's head moved slowly from side to side; her eyes stayed closed. "Co. . .come. . .station. Dark. Duty."

Though she understood the words, Julie could not make sense of what her grandmother muttered.

೨ಾ

Tree-lined countryside gave way to concrete walls and red brick buildings towering above her. The train rumbled along the tracks, slowing gradually once it was within the city limits. Finally it lurched to a stop, the breaks giving off a high-pitched hoarse whistle.

Julienne Leed had arrived in Chicago.

She watched as the passengers around her rose, gathered their belongings, and headed purposefully down the narrow aisle. She ought to have been doing the same thing, but she did not move. Her decision to leave Maine slapped her hard. With her family—her parents and three younger brothers— Julienne had traveled around New England on numerous occasions. But this was different. This was not a visit, not an exploratory trip. And it was a final decision.

After finishing one semester of nurses' training in Chicago, Julienne had returned home for the summer. Her mother had spent the entire three months disparaging Julienne's decision to train as a nurse. She fully expected Julienne to get her noble ambitions out of her system and return to a more regulated life, one that followed her own expectations more closely.

The departure scene on that September morning had been horrible. Julienne's mother refused even to come to the train station to see her off. In fact, she had caused such a ruckus standing on the porch of Leed House that Julienne had nearly missed her train. As much as her mother frustrated her—and always had—she had hoped for an amicable parting.

But it was not to be, and now Julienne had arrived in Chicago to resume her studies, firmly convinced that she must choose her family or her future career. At stake, really, was the right to make her own choices. Her mother had put her foot down and chased away the one thing that Julienne had ever chosen: Lorenzo Scorzo. Julienne had loved Lorenzo as much as a girl her age could love a man. But her mother had made sure he went away. Julienne was determined that her mother would not make another choice for her.

Though she would never admit it to her mother, doubt about her nursing training seared through Julienne nearly every day. It was far more tedious academic work than had been demanded of her during her school years. And even though she was a student, her exposure to the hospital rang like a gong in her head. Her comfortable, rural New England upbringing had not prepared her for the suffering she saw at a downtown hospital in a city as big as Chicago. Seeing the children was the most wrenching part. . .the children brought in by parents who waited until it was almost too late because they could not afford a doctor's fee. Or the children who lived in squalor and never knew anything different. She could not help thinking of her own little brothers at those times, her robust, noisy brothers who annoyed her to no end but whom she loved dearly.

The passenger car was empty now, except for Julienne. With mixed feelings she stood up, straightened her gray skirt, and adjusted the tilt of her best hat. She grabbed hold of her heavy bag, heaved, and started down the aisle. Progress was slow as she lugged the bag one step at a time. She came to the metal stairs at the back of the car. Reinforcing her grip on the bag, she started down.

Julienne had waited so long to get off the train that the crowd on the platform had thinned out. The rush to recover trunks from the luggage car had passed. In the early evening only a few isolated figures dotted the platform. One of them moved toward her. She turned to meet his eyes.

"I thought perhaps you would not come back," he said, reaching for her bag.

"I knew I had to," she answered gravely.

He offered his arm and she took it. "We'll ask them to deliver your trunk to the dormitory," he said.

She nodded and let him lead the way. He stopped for a moment to give instructions to a porter about the trunk and then continued out to the street.

"Are you sure you don't mind walking?" he asked. "I could try to hire a cab."

She shook her head. "I need to stretch my legs after that train ride. I'd like to walk."

They did not speak for a long time after that. Colin Covington and Julienne Leed had come to a comfortable friendship some months ago. It was Colin who had encouraged her to apply to nursing school in the first place. He knew all about Lorenzo and never expected anything of Julienne beyond friendship. It was comforting to be able to walk down the street and not have to explain herself.

Over the summer, Julienne had realized something about Colin Covington. She had missed him a lot, much more than she had expected to when he put her on a train last June. More than that, she realized that she missed him precisely because he asked so little of her. Slowly, over the course of the summer weeks, she had realized that Colin Covington simply accepted her. Painfully, she acknowledged that he was the only person in her life to do so.

They arrived at her dormitory building and he looked at her

awkwardly as they stood outside the door.

"I always feel odd coming to this place," he said.

"Why?"

"I feel out of place, as if I'm somewhere I don't belong."

"I assure you the housemother will let you know if that happens." She paused, not sure what to do now. "Do you want to sit in the lobby for a few minutes. . .perhaps catch up on the news of the summer?" Her voice had a strangely hopeful tone she did not mean for it to have.

He glanced at his watch. "I go on duty in about an hour. But I've got time for a cup of coffee."

Julienne tentatively opened the heavy front door of the dormitory and scanned the lobby. A couple of classmates sat at a table playing a game. In the corner, the large coffee urn brewed coffee, emitting a rich, dark, familiar aroma. She turned and looked at him over her shoulder.

"Everything's the same as I left it," she said with satisfaction. The matching damask, camel-back sofas sat on each side of the brick fireplace. Dark walnut tables accented the room, with lamps softly glowing atop lace doilies.

"Will you have the same room?"

"I think so. I requested it last spring. It has such lovely light in the morning."

He smiled, sharing her pleasure though he had never seen the morning light in her room. It was enough to see her happy.

"Why don't you see if Mrs. Davis is in and pick up your room key?" he asked.

"That can wait. I'll get you a cup of coffee."

She wiggled her fingers in greeting at the two young women at the game table and then went to the coffee urn. She filled two tin cups to the brim and balanced them carefully as she made her way back to the couch where Colin sat. She smiled inwardly. He did look nervous. He probably did not even realize his left knee was twitching at regular intervals.

"Here you go, strong and black, the way you like it." She handed him a cup. "Sorry about those awful cups. We keep asking Mrs. Davis to get some decent dishes, but she likes the fact that these will last forever."

Colin shrugged. The cups did not matter to him. He blew across the top of the steaming liquid. "How is your family?" he asked.

She did not know if he was being polite or sincere, so she was unsure of how to answer him. She rolled her eyes slightly. "The same. Mother is running everyone's life and Father is letting her."

He nodded knowingly. They had had similar discussions many times.

"Of course, Mother wanted me to stay home," Julienne continued, "but I couldn't do that. Not anymore." She paused and then said quietly, "I'm not sure Leed House is home anymore."

Colin took a sip of coffee and looked at her with steady gray eyes. "That's a choice for each of us to make."

Julienne felt a lump in her throat and decided to change the subject. She set her cup down. "You have duty at the hospital. I don't want to make you late."

He took her hint and swallowed the last of his coffee. "Right."

"Will you be on duty all night?"

"I'm afraid so. The life of an intern."

"Thanks for meeting my train."

"It was my pleasure." He rose to leave. "I'll let you get settled in and call you in a couple of days to see if you need anything.

She nodded her thanks as they moved toward the door. Just as she closed it behind him, she heard the cheery voice of

Mrs. Davis, the housemother given charge of the young nursing students.

"Why, Julienne Leed, you decided to come back after all."

Julienne turned to smile at Mrs. Davis. "I just couldn't stay away from you."

"Flattery will get you nowhere. Now take that bag of yours and go upstairs. I'll bring the key."

⁂

"Col. Col. Where Col." The old woman muttered restlessly and her granddaughter patted her hand.

"It's okay, Grammy. You're fine." Then it dawned on her what the nearly inaudible sounds meant. Col. Colin. Grammy was calling for her husband, who had died more than twenty years ago.

"You're lonely, aren't you, Grammy?"

The old woman slipped back into sleep.

"I wish I could remember everything you ever told me about him," Julie whispered.

The door opened and her mother stuck her head into the room. "There you are. Want some breakfast? I'm making waffles."

four

"I think we all agree it's time we did something about this situation." Julie's Aunt Jane made her announcement without fanfare as she looked around the dining room table. The occasion was a formal family forum. The topic was what to do about Grammy. Julie sat sullenly at one end of the long table; Aunt Jane sat at the opposite end. On the one hand, Julie did not want to be a part of this discussion at all. On the other hand, she did not trust any other members of her family to make Grammy the priority in their decision.

Her parents would try to do what was best for her grandmother. Julie felt sure of that. But they were worn out. Her peacekeeping father, Tom, had taken Grammy in to stop the squabbling of his sisters, Jane and Fran. But it had been a temporary solution; everyone knew that the time would come when Grammy would need more care than they could give. And now that time had come. Tom and Liz Covington were tired, perhaps too tired to do anything other than go along with whatever Jane decreed.

Jane and Fran were of one mind: Grammy was a problem that had to be solved, a situation to remedy, a task to assign.

She's their mother, Julie thought to herself over and over. How can they treat her with so little compassion? She would never be satisfied with any defense they gave of their actions.

Marjorie sat next to Julie, drumming her fingers on the polished table top. As usual, she wanted a quick decision. Saturdays were busy days and a long list of activities awaited her attention. The sooner a decision was made, the better.

Julie's only hope for alliance was her brother, and that was a slim one. He was too much like his father. Though he cared for Grammy more genuinely than the rest, he was not by nature a strong person. He would go along with what seemed expedient to avoid conflict and then try to make the best of the situation.

Jane and Fran would get what they wanted; that much was clear already. Still, waves of protest welled up within Julie.

"I'm sure we can come to a quick decision in this situation," Fran said, looking around the table for agreement.

"Grammy is not a 'situation.' She's your mother." Julie's tone was bitter.

Fran ignored her remark. "Jane and I have looked at several nursing homes in the area. They are quite suitable and two of them have bed space available right now."

"Bed space?" Julie questioned. "Is that how you're measuring Grammy's welfare?"

"Julie," Marjorie said sternly. "You have to stop interrupting. Maybe you shouldn't be here."

"I have as much right to be here as you!"

"Of course you do. But you don't want to face the fact that this has to be done."

"I know we have to do this," Julie said, looking around the table. "But I can't help thinking that you're going to choose what's convenient for you instead of what's really best for Grammy."

"And just what do you think is really best for Grammy?" one of her cousins challenged.

Julie did not like the sneering tone behind the question, but she struggled to answer it. "I want Grammy to be somewhere that she will be treated as a person, not a problem. I know she's difficult to deal with and likely to get worse. But why does everyone have to focus on that?"

"You were gone all summer," said Marjorie, a hint of accusation filtering through her words. "You don't know what things were like around here."

Julie cocked her head defiantly. "That's because no one told me."

"I called you several times." Her mother's voice was quiet and fragile. "You never seemed to want to talk."

Julie had no response. It was true. She had deliberately distanced herself from her family while she was in Maine.

"How Julie spent her summer is not the question right now." Aunt Jane was impatient. She looked at Julie directly. "We all appreciate your special relationship with your grandmother. You are the last grandchild. But I assure you we all want what's best for her, and we really must make a decision soon."

Julie looked down at her hands in her lap while Fran continued her presentation of the options. She described the facilities of both nursing homes, the ratio between nurses and patients, the costs, and a lot of other details that Julie lost track of. An hour later the consensus was that Grammy should enter the Prairie Valley Nursing Center and that the move could be accomplished within two weeks. Julie was silent throughout the discussion. In the end, she was glad that at least they had selected the option that was closest to home, rather than the one that was an hour's drive away.

The room emptied out. Jane and Fran made a quick, efficient list of what they needed to do to arrange the move. Ted gave Julie a look that said, "I know you feel bad but I can't do anything about it," then he left. Marjorie rattled on about soccer practice and piano lessons and was soon gone. Tom and Liz retreated into the kitchen. In a few moments, Julie smelled the fragrance of a fresh pot of coffee brewing.

Julie could picture her parents, sitting at the kitchen table, as they often did, drinking coffee and conversing in low, thoughtful tones. It had been their habit for as long as she could remember. Her mother's earlier words, "You never seemed to want to talk," played over and over in Julie's mind.

All summer long, Julie had resisted what she thought was her mother's interference in her life. Her mother had not wanted her to go to Maine in the first place. At the time, Julie thought her mother was being overprotective. Now, she thought differently. Had her mother been reaching out to her all that time, looking for someone who truly understood the burden she carried in caring for her mother-in-law? Julie put a hand to her mouth to stifle a cry of guilt. How could she have been so blind to the signals her mother was sending?

She stood up and walked toward the swinging door to the kitchen. Pushing it open, she stood there, unsure of what to do next.

Tom Covington looked up at his youngest child, a question in his eyes. "Julie?"

She choked on her response and looked at her mother, then back at her father.

"Is something wrong, Julie?" her mother asked. "I know the family meeting was hard for you, but—"

Julie shook her head. "It's not that." She swallowed with difficulty. "I'm sorry about the summer, Mom. I treated you badly."

Liz Covington got up and put her arms around her daughter. "It's a hard time for all of us," she said, "but by God's grace we'll get through it."

"Thanks, Mom." She turned to her father. "Dad, can I ask you something?"

"Sure, what?"

"Why didn't you ever go to Seabridge when you were growing up?" Julie settled into a chair across from her father.

Tom was obviously surprised by the question.

"Both of your parents came from there," Julie continued. "It seems odd that you never went back."

Tom poured himself more coffee. "It was hard for my father to get away from his practice when I was little. But his parents came to visit us twice every year."

"But what about Grammy's parents? Did you know them?"

Tom shook his head. "Not as well. I can remember overhearing my parents talking about Grandma Leed, and she visited a couple of times. I never knew what was wrong, but she and my mother didn't seem to get along."

Julie nodded, remembering the diary's story of how Lorenzo had been chased away. She could not help wondering if that is why her grandmother had never reconciled with her own family.

"I want to help get Grammy settled," Julie said, bringing her thoughts back to the present.

Her mother smiled knowingly. "I'm sure you realize Jane and Fran will have it all arranged."

Julie laughed nervously. "All the more reason for me to be there."

Both her parents chuckled.

"If you're sure you want to put yourself through that," her father said. "I'd like to think your grandmother would appreciate it."

Julie nodded. "I want to do it." She pushed out a cleansing breath. "Well, I guess I'd better get back to school. Dennis has tickets to a concert tonight."

"Tell him hello," her mother said, "and bring him home for dinner sometime soon."

"I will." She glanced toward the living room. "I'll just go say goodbye to Grammy and then get my stuff together."

five

"How is she?" Julie asked. On an impulse she had decided to drive home for dinner on Tuesday night and check on her grandmother. She scrubbed potatoes next to her mother at the sink and asked the questions on her mind.

"Does she have any idea of what's happening?"

Liz Covington shrugged her shoulders. "It's hard to tell. Sometimes she looks at me so directly that I think she can understand what I'm saying. Other times, her face is blank and I don't know where she is."

"I wish there were a way to get through to her," Julie mumbled.

"It wouldn't matter. If she knew she was being put in a nursing home, she'd throw a fit. Maybe it's better this way."

"But, Mom, she reacts to things. She doesn't always understand, or at least can't communicate what she knows, but she reacts emotionally."

Julie's mother was nodding. "I know. That's what the fits are all about, I suppose. But what is she reacting to? What's happening now or something that she's remembering?"

"What do you mean?"

"She mumbles a lot. You've heard her. But she's saying real words and sometimes whole sentences. Today she said, 'The park was fun, Colin,' clear as a bell." Liz scraped the carrots with extra vigor. "And she's been in a great mood, just grinning from ear to ear. I just don't know what to make of it when she does things like that."

"So you think the fits are bad memories?"

"Just a theory." Liz opened the refrigerator and began unloading salad ingredients. "How about you fix the salad?"

At the dinner table, Julie helped feed her grandmother, guiding the hands that grabbed food randomly, wiping the chin when the food would not stay in her mouth. Grammy was peaceful but tired. As soon as she was finished eating, Julie took her upstairs and put her to bed. She sat there, holding the old woman's hand until she fell asleep, a mysterious smile on her face.

❧

The city sidewalks gave way to leisurely lanes, squarish houses with manicured lawns, and open fields.

Julienne pressed her face to the train window like a little girl. The train ride was not new, but the scenery was. They were rattling away from Chicago, out to Marksville, a small town west of Chicago. Over the summer a new amusement park had opened up. Colin insisted that Julienne should see it before the end of the season, which was only two weeks away.

Julienne had been back at school for a month already. She had hardly seen Colin at all. His internship schedule left him virtually no free time, but he had finagled a whole Saturday off to take her out to Marksville. She had nearly declined his invitation; she usually counted on the weekends to catch up on her studies. But he had pleaded so earnestly and gone to so much trouble to get the day off. How could she refuse?

School was not going well. Academically she was in good shape—near the top of her class, in fact. But fear of the future gnawed at her every day. Was she really cut out to help hurting people? Even looking at diagrams in her textbooks sometimes made her squeamish. And when she had to observe a procedure at the hospital, it took every ounce of concentration she had not to run out of the room. Would she ever develop the instincts to react to a crisis? Could she set aside her own feelings to concentrate completely on someone else?

Julienne glanced across the seat at Colin. So far he knew nothing of these misgivings. She felt like she was keeping a secret from her best friend. That was really what Colin had become—her best friend. Without any romantic involvement, they were comfortable together discussing a variety of topics. Most of the time she confided in him freely. She was glad to have a friend, especially one who knew and understood her heartbreak over losing Lorenzo only a year ago. It would be a long time before Julienne would be ready to think about romance again. At least being in nursing school gave her something on which to focus. But was she there for the wrong reasons, simply to escape her own fears and hurts?

If only the nagging doubts would subside. It had been Colin's suggestion that she come to Chicago to go to school in the first place. He would feel responsible if he knew she was even the least bit unhappy. So she had not told him. Besides, she absolutely did not want to go back to Maine and give her mother the satisfaction of being right.

"It shouldn't be too much longer." Colin's voice startled her. It had been a long time since either of them had spoken.

She gave him a wan smile. "The countryside is pretty out here. So different from Maine."

Colin nodded. "I think that's part of why I enjoy taking the ride out here. It's different even from Chicago. So close and yet so far." He looked out the window and sat up straight. "There's the river now."

"What river?"

"The Fox River. This is the Marksville stop."

The tracks now ran parallel to the green water, crisscrossing the bridge that carried traffic over the river. They were in the downtown area. The train slowed to a halt. Julie questioned Colin with her eyes.

"Not here," he said. "There's a stop closer to the park."

She settled back in her seat for a few more minutes. As Colin followed their route with his eyes, Julienne studied him for a quick moment. His face was bright and his eyes were full of boyish expectancy. He was dressed in gray flannel slacks and a blue cotton sweater. She was used to seeing him in a white medical smock with a stethoscope dangling around his neck. He had a habit of hiding his hands in the oversized patch pockets of the smock, fingering the fountain pen that he always kept handy, often being deep in thought. But there was none of that today. Along with taking the day off, he had left his medical identity behind. Today he was a young man who had left his cares behind and had become a boy again. Julienne envied his ability to do that.

"Here we are," he said as the train came to another stop. He stood up and offered his arm. "Ready?"

"Ready." She linked her arm through his and, with hundreds of other passengers, they stepped off the train and into the world of Treasure Cove Amusement Park.

Julienne nearly gasped at what she saw. She should have been paying more attention to Colin's enthusiastic description; maybe then she would have been prepared for what she saw. The carousel, the ferris wheel, the arcade games, the cotton candy—it was a magical kingdom. Carnivals never came to her small hometown in New England and her parents steadfastly held the opinion that they were a frivolous waste of time and money, so the family never made the trip to a nearby town at carnival time. Julienne's childhood friend, Joanna, had been allowed to go and always came home starry-eyed. Now Julienne understood why.

"What do you want to do first?" Colin's voice carried a pitch of energy. He was ready to do it all.

"I'm. . .I'm not quite sure," Julienne answered as she stood just inside the entry gate and soaked in her surroundings. There were people everywhere, thousands of them: children squealing their delight on the rides; parents nagging children not to eat too much; older people sitting on benches and watching the scene with pleasure.

"I can't believe you never went to the carnival," Colin said. "One came through every couple of years. My family always went."

"When my mother makes up her mind, she doesn't change it." She gestured widely around her. "This is wonderful. Just what I needed today. Thanks for bringing me."

"My pleasure." He grabbed her hand and pulled on it. "Come on, let's do the ferris wheel. From the top you can see the whole park. Then you can choose where to go next."

Julienne looked skeptical but said, "All right. The ferris wheel it is."

The line was long but moving steadily. While they stood in it, Julienne listened to the music being cranked out around them. She heard at least three different tunes being played by various rides and couldn't decide what to concentrate on. When she glanced at Colin, he looked more carefree than she had ever seen him. Awkwardly she realized he was still holding her hand. It had seemed so natural when he grabbed it, but now, looking at their fingers laced together, surprise struck. Colin had never held her hand before.

Sensing her self-consciousness, Colin released his hold. "It's almost our turn," he said.

In a few minutes they were seated in the green bucketlike compartment of the ferris wheel. When another three cars had been loaded, the wheel began to spin. Julienne felt her stomach leap as they went over the top curve and started on the way down. Each time they reached the top again, she tried to look in a different direction out over the park.

The hours passed quickly that day. They rode every ride in sight. Colin won two stuffed animals at the arcade games; Julienne ate cotton candy three times, at which point Colin insisted that she eat some real food. As they slumped into chairs at an outdoor cafe, Julienne laid her head back, content.

Colin smiled at her. "You look like you're enjoying the day."

"I am! I can't believe I almost didn't come."

"Then it pays for me to be persistent with you." He reached across the table and patted her hand.

Her only response was to smile.

"You seem relaxed," Colin observed.

She nodded. "I hate to admit it, but I really needed this break."

He laughed lightly. "But you've been back to school for only a month. Surely you're not studied out already."

Julienne shook her head. "No, I can study all right." She hesitated to say more. When she spoke it was in a low voice. "I haven't communicated with my mother since I got back. I keep hoping she'll change her mind about what I'm doing."

Colin took both of her hands in his. "Julienne, the important thing is that you are doing what you think you should be doing. I know you gave a lot of thought, and prayer, to the decision to enter nursing school. Don't underestimate your ability to make a decision."

She shrugged one shoulder. "I'm not used to making decisions."

"Well, practice on small things." Colin withdrew his hands and sat up straight. "The next thing you have to decide is what you want to eat."

Relieved that he had not pressed her further, she turned her attention to the menu and ordered a cold chicken salad. When it arrived, she ate voraciously, as if the three cotton candies had never existed. She pushed her empty plate away and realized, a little embarrassed, that Colin was still eating. She had practically swallowed her food without bothering to chew.

"Has anyone ever told you that you should take your time when you eat?" Colin teased.

"Only this doctor friend of mind," she retorted. "But what does he know about a woman's hunger?"

He laughed. "Not much, I guess."

"What time does the train leave? Do we have time for one more ride on the carousel?"

Still smiling, he nodded. "Sure."

She met his smile with her own. They had not talked much during the day, but something had happened between then. When he finished eating, he stood up and offered his hand. She took it without hesitation.

෴

Julie gently slipped her hand out of her grandmother's sleeping grip. Mom was right, she decided. Grammy does look like she's had a good day. If only every day could be like this.

She closed the door gently behind her and padded down the carpeted stairs to the family room, where her parents sat, reading the newspaper.

"Is she down for the night?" Tom Covington asked.

"I think so. She seemed very peaceful. Almost happy."

"See what I mean?" Liz said.

Julie nodded. "I'd better get back to school. I still have to work on an English paper tonight."

"How's Dennis?"

The question took Julie by surprise. She had not really thought about Dennis much that day. "Actually I haven't seen him today. But it's still early. We'll probably talk tonight."

"Well, give him our love."

"I will." She leaned over and kissed both her parents. "Good night. I'll see you on Saturday."

She left right after that. Her mother's innocent question about Dennis haunted her. She could have brought Dennis home for dinner, too, but she had not thought about it at the time. In fact, she had not thought about Dennis all day. She had not seen him in two days. She seemed to miss his phone calls and had not made much of an effort to catch up with him.

All I can think about is Grammy, she told herself. Once we get her settled, I'll be able to pay more attention to Dennis.

The truth was she was not so sure.

six

Julie took a gulp of cold water and moved her eyes back to the beginning of the paragraph. Three previous attempts to read the same section of her sociology textbook had failed. Each time her mind wandered off on some tangent. She would find herself preoccupied with her grandmother or her mother or her sister, Marjorie. But she faced a quiz later that afternoon on this chapter, so she was determined to get through the material, despite her difficulties with concentration.

The library was quiet in the middle of the day. Behind her a student worker was reshelving books. At the next table a senior was working on an honors project. Many of the students were in class or at lunch—which Julie was skipping in order to cram for the quiz. She was beginning to think she might just as well have gone to lunch, since she was not absorbing information too well just then. She looked at the chart at the bottom of the page and tried to memorize it. Squeezing her eyes shut, she tried to picture the information in the chart. Some of it floated before her, but not all of it.

She did not hear the sound behind her, so she jumped a little when two hands covered her eyes. She recognized the touch and relaxed.

"Hello, Dennis," she said. He released her and she turned in her chair and looked up at him. She whispered, "I tried to call you last night."

"Sorry about that. I've had some irons in the fire, so I've been busy." He fell into a chair next to her and scooted it closer so they could keep their voices low.

"What's going on?" Dennis was always good natured, but Julie was not sure of what to make of the extra big smile on his face today.

"Have you ever thought about living somewhere else?" he whispered playfully.

She looked at his eyes, questioning.

"Some place like Seattle," he continued.

Her eyes grew wide. "Seattle? That's two thousand miles away."

Dennis nodded. "I know. But I just got a pretty enticing job offer out there." He reached into his shirt pocket and pulled out a crumpled envelope. "Take a look at this."

Slowly, nervously, Julie opened up the envelope and unfolded the letter. She scanned the letter, written in perfect business English. An established manufacturing company was expanding their computer capabilities. Dennis would get to head up the project. When Julie saw the salary figure, her eyes bulged and her jaw dropped. She looked at him in disbelief.

"Pretty incredible, huh?" Dennis said, still grinning.

"I thought you already had two job offers in Chicago." Julie was confused. She had not known Dennis was job hunting in other parts of the country.

"I do. But not like this. Even apart from the salary, this is a dream job for a computer junkie like me. Troubleshooting, writing new programs. . .I'd get to do it all."

"Sounds perfect." She handed the letter back to him. "Are you going to take it?"

Dennis grew somber and leaned in toward her. "Look, Julie, I know we agreed not to talk about marriage for six months, but this changes things. I want you to be part of this decision if there is any chance that we're ever going to get married."

"Oh, Dennis. . ." Julie did not know what to say. "It's a

chance of lifetime for someone just out of college. If it's what you want, I think you should do it."

"You're avoiding the question, Julie."

She rolled her eyes slightly and slapped her pencil down a little too hard. "We're in the middle of the library and I'm supposed to be cramming for a sociology quiz." Her hoarse whisper held a hint of irritation.

Dennis persisted. "I would think you'd be thrilled to be able to spend all your time painting without having to worry about money." He was definitely getting annoyed.

"This has nothing to do with money!" Julie retorted, her voice rising above a whisper.

"Shhhh." The warning came from the student worker shelving books nearby.

Julie lowered her voice. "I can't give you an answer about marriage right on the spot."

"Well, it's not like we've never discussed it before."

"But we agreed to stop discussing it for a while."

Dennis put his elbows on his knees and hung his head in his hands. "Okay. I was reluctant to agree to that, but I did, so I have to live with it."

Julie looked at Dennis thoughtfully. His sandy hair that would not stay combed and his wide grin were always inviting, even endearing. They had been dating for over two years and they knew each other inside out. She was comfortable with Dennis and depended on him for a lot of things. But when he talked about getting married, something always made her hesitant. If she tried to analyze the situation logically, all indications were that she should marry Dennis and have a very pleasant life. He would earn more than enough money for them to live on, and she would be free to paint, maybe even open a studio. But somehow that was not enough.

She reached out and touched his hand. "Congratulations

on the job offer, Dennis. It's wonderful. I'm proud of you and genuinely happy for you." She meant what she was saying.

He stood up without returning her gesture. "We'll talk later, I guess. I'd better let you get back to cramming."

"How about dinner tonight?"

"Meet you at the dining hall at six o'clock." She expected him to kiss her before he left, but he did not.

Julie looked blandly at the textbook in front of her and then at her watch. Once again she moved her eyes to the paragraph at the top of the page and forced herself to read slowly and deliberately. She read two pages this way before stopping. Nothing was sinking in.

It was hopeless. She would never get that amount of information into her brain in such a limited amount of time. If she was having trouble concentrating before, Dennis's announcement had put her over the edge. She would just have to go on what she had already studied. She closed the textbook and her notebook and started stuffing her belongings into a canvas book bag. Another glance at her watch told her that there might still be a chance to get lunch in the cafeteria. With her bag slung over her shoulder, she started the trek across the gently rolling hills of the campus.

Out of a side path a familiar figure emerged. "Hi, Melanie," Julie greeted her roommate. "Ready for the quiz?"

Melanie grimaced. "Dr. Robbins has a pretty stiff reputation. I don't know what to expect." She fell into step beside Julie. "Hey, I took a phone message for you a little while ago."

"Oh? My mother?"

"No. Some guy. Said his name was Larry and he would call again later."

Julie nearly stopped in her tracks. Why would Larry be calling her? "Larry? Was it long distance?"

"Sounded like it. Someone you know?"

Julie nodded. "Someone I met in Maine this summer, but I can't imagine why he'd be calling me."

"Well, he did and he will again."

"Thanks for the message." Julie waved as Melanie branched off on the path leading to the science labs.

The dining hall was nearly empty so late in the lunch period. Julie was glad. She was not really in the mood for making conversation with a table full of students. She sat in a booth by herself and concentrated on her soup and sandwich.

Two hours later the quiz was over her and Julie was relieved. Not one of her shining efforts. But then, she was only in the class because she needed the general credits for graduation. Maybe if she were more interested in sociology she would not have had such a problem studying. Leaving the classroom with a sigh, Julie turned her face to the autumn sun and felt the soft breeze ripple her blond hair. The day was a gentle one, warm but without the intensity of the summer's heat, and refreshing without bordering on blustery. Even the light seemed softer than a few weeks ago, less intense, more fluid.

Julie decided she had enough time to head back to her dorm to freshen up before meeting Dennis for supper. They had been going along comfortably enough as two students at the same school. Now, with the job offer pending, there would be a wedge building between them until they decided something about the future. More accurately, it was up to her to decide something about the future. Dennis had made his intentions clear over and over again. Julie was the one who could not commit herself.

As she entered the suite where her room was, the phone in the hall was ringing. No one else seemed to be around, so on the fourth ring she picked up the phone. "Hello," she said.

"Julie Covington, please."

"This is Julie. Larry? Is that you?"

"Yes! Hi, Julie. Glad I caught you." He sounded cheerful, increasing Julie's curiosity about why he was calling.

"Is everything all right? Is Della okay?"

"Mom's fine," he assured her. "Are you?"

Julie was uncertain of how to answer such a question coming from Larry. Her relationship with him during the summer had been casual. Though she had been curiously attracted to him, he had made it clear that theirs was only a light friendship. Her bond had really been with his mother, Della.

She struggled for words. "I'm fine, too. Things are a little tough at home right now, but I think it'll work out. What can I do for you?"

"Please don't feel you have to do anything for me. I was hesitant to bother you, but Mom insisted I call."

"Why?"

"I'm coming to Chicago. I think she wants me to check up on you, make sure you're really all right."

Was she understanding him correctly? Did he want to see her? "When are you coming?" she asked.

"In two weeks. There's a trade show at McCormick Place for operators of small hotels."

"How long will you be here?"

"Four days. I told Mom you would be busy with school, so don't feel you have to rearrange your schedule. But it would make her happy if I saw you and could give her a firsthand report."

"Actually, I don't have any classes on Wednesday. I could probably get away during the day. But won't you be tied up at the convention?"

"The schedule's pretty flexible. Would it be hard for me to find my way out to Lovellton?"

"There's a train every three hours or so from downtown Chicago."

"Great. Why don't I give you a call when I get to Chicago and we can nail down a plan then."

"That would be great. I look forward to seeing you. Too bad Della won't be with you."

"Someone has to hold down the fort."

"Thanks for calling."

She hung up the phone, hardly believing what had just happened. She had left Maine only a couple of months ago. She certainly had not expected to see Larry Paxton again so soon—if ever. Now he was coming all the way to Lovellton.

Panic struck. What would she do with Larry Paxton for a day? Her mind whirred, considering the options. Actually they were few. Lovellton was not a very exciting place. There was no scenic coastline, no historic homes, nothing of the charm of Seabridge, Maine. Julie chided herself for not saying she would meet him in Chicago, where there would be more to see.

She tried to recall the train schedule. He would want to avoid the commuter runs, so he probably wouldn't stay long anyway. Perhaps they could just go somewhere for lunch.

Julie calmed herself with that thought. Just lunch. She could manage that. And after all, her good friend Della was the one sending Larry on this mission. Julie would go to extra lengths to make Della happy, and Larry would, too, she knew. So that's what they would do: make Della happy by having a short visit.

Still standing in the hall with her book bag on her shoulder, Julie fumbled in a pants pocket for her room key. The lock was temperamental—and irritating—but even in her nervousness she got it open. She dropped her book bag with a thud and fell backwards onto the bed, her arms stretched out over her head. What a day. Between the quiz and Dennis and Larry, nothing had gone the way she had expected when she got up that morning. Somehow she had to get her life back under control.

She got off the bed and stood in front of the dresser, inspecting her image in the mirror. Her hair had not received any serious attention in days. It was simpler just to pull it back in a big clip to keep it out of her face as she studied. Her clothes were rumpled; it was too much trouble to set up an ironing board in a dorm room. Under her eyes hung dark bluish bags, evidence that she had not been sleeping well.

"Covington, you're a wreck," she said aloud to herself. With one hand she released the brass clip in her hair and with the other she scooped up a hairbrush off the dresser. Maybe if she looked better she would feel better when she met Dennis for dinner.

seven

"You're sure getting a lot of calls lately," Melanie said, as she held the receiver out for Julie the next day.

Julie took the phone from her roommate. "Can't help it if I'm popular."

"Sounds like your mom," Melanie stated as she disappeared around the corner into their room.

"Mom?"

"Hi, Julie. How are you?"

"I've had better days, but I'm okay. What's up?"

"Your Aunt Jane just called to say that it really is not necessary for you to come along when we take Grammy."

"Mom—" Julie started to protest.

"I know, honey," her mother said soothingly, "you want to be there and I think you should be. I just thought you should know that there might be some opposition when the time comes."

Julie was silent for a moment, trying to suppress her irritation. "I'm going to focus on Grammy. Aunt Jane has nothing to worry about. I'll stay out of her way."

"That's just what I told her."

"Maybe Aunt Jane is the one who doesn't need to be there. If she's made all the arrangements, she's already done her part."

It was her mother's turn to be silent.

"Mom?"

"I'm all right. You might be right about Jane, but somehow I think she will insist on being there."

Julie sighed. "Well, thanks for the warning. I'll stop in sometime over the weekend."

"I could tell you that's not necessary, but it wouldn't matter."

"That's right."

"I'll see you in a few days, then."

Julie put the phone on its hook and leaned her forehead against the wall. "I'm there for you, Grammy," she muttered, "no matter what anyone says."

"Julie?"

She turned to see Melanie standing in the hall.

"Something wrong? Is it your grandmother?"

"Everything's okay, I guess. It's just kind of a tough time." Julie gave her friend a forced smile and headed back to the stack of books on her desk.

❧

Julienne twirled the ice cream cone in her hands and licked the top scoop unabashedly. She smiled up at Colin, walking beside her. "How did you know I had the afternoon free?" she asked.

"A little birdie told me that the nurses' classes had been unexpectedly cancelled today."

She nodded. "Surprised us all. The instructor was sick and they couldn't get anyone to replace her. Guess things are pretty busy around the hospital."

Colin handed her his handkerchief. "You need this."

Embarrassed, she dabbed at the corners of her mouth before continuing her assault on the double dip delight. "I really should be home studying."

"And you will be. But if I can break away from the hospital for an hour, so can you."

She nodded contentedly. It wasn't as though she really wanted to be in her room with a pile of books. It was a beautiful late

October day. A cold snap in the weather had quickly retreated and left renewed warmth in its wake. Grateful for a brief reprise of summer, the neighborhood people filled the streets around the hospital. Children were swinging with sticks at rocks on the sidewalk while their mothers sat on front stoops up and down the street in an attempt to escape the stale air inside their apartments.

"Are you sure you can't get the rest of the day off?" Julienne was ready to play hookey for several hours.

"Sorry. I have to do pediatric rounds this afternoon," Colin answered.

"Have you made up your mind to specialize in pediatrics?" She caught a drop of ice cream just before it oozed over her hand.

He nodded. "I think that is where I am meant to be."

Silently she envied his confidence. If only she had a fraction of the certainty he had. "How can you be so sure?"

He shrugged. "I figure God made me the way I am for a reason. I try to figure what I'm good at and see what He wants me to do with it."

"That's easy for you. You have lots of talents. It's not so simple for me."

"I wish you would stop belittling yourself," Colin said. "God gave you plenty of talents, too."

"I'm not so sure." Julienne was unconvinced.

Their reflective conversation was interrupted by a commotion on the sidewalk ahead of them.

"Thomas Edison MacEnzie!" One mother jumped to her feet and pointed at a second-story window. "You get your head inside that room right this minute."

Julienne was fleetingly amused. A mother was a mother everywhere. But then she looked in horror at the small boy reaching farther out the window for a toy stuck on the ledge.

In a fraction of a second he had leaned out too far, lost his balance, and landed on the sidewalk thirty feet in front of her. His mother screamed.

Colin bolted ahead and knelt over the crumpled boy. Julienne followed closely, holding her breath as Colin did a quick examination. Within seconds, they were hemmed in by a crowd of spectators.

"Give me room to work, please," Colin shouted. "I'm a doctor." He laid his head against the boy's chest. "Quiet, please!" The crowd hushed just long enough for him to hear what he listened for. He sighed heavily, then pushed the child's eyelids open to examine his pupils.

"Colin?" Julienne's voice was hushed and frightened.

Colin turned to the boy's mother. "He's alive, but he's unconscious. There are several broken bones, and probably internal bleeding. We must get him to the hospital immediately."

"But I have no money for the hospital," the anguished mother said.

Colin continued his assessment. "We should try not to move him any more than necessary." He turned to Julienne. "I think we should have a stretcher from the hospital."

She did not move, but just looked at him without understanding.

"Go, Julienne!" he urged. "We're only a block from the hospital. Get a stretcher and some help!"

His eyes pleaded with her to respond, and she wanted to, but somehow her arms and legs would not move. Finally, she unfroze. "Right. A stretcher. I'll be right back."

Ten minutes later, Colin burst through the side doors of the hospital, trotting alongside the stretcher carriers. Julienne trailed behind.

"Over here," a nurse called out. Colin pointed to the left and led the way. The boy was quickly transferred to the examination table. Colin took his pulse and listened to his shallow, quick breaths. "Hang on, Thomas Edison MacEnzie," he whispered. "Don't leave us now." Nurses peeled off the boy's torn clothing and Colin examined his abdomen carefully and gingerly. "There's definitely some internal bleeding and at least two broken ribs on the left side. And his left leg is broken in two places."

Julienne was only a student nurse. She had been trained to help with a few simple procedures but was not prepared for the frantic pace of an emergency. She cowered in the corner near the entrance, scrambling to make sense of everything she saw. Colin confidently called out orders, and experienced nurses and technicians efficiently followed his bidding. But Julienne was in a fog, numb, hardly able to make sense of what she saw. The boy could not have been more than six years old, younger than her littlest brother. He lay there pale and breathing with difficulty. It frightened her that he remained unconscious. Periodically she caught Colin checking his eyes again and again. She knew he was looking for a glimmer of response.

Suddenly Julienne remembered the mother. She turned back to the waiting room and scanned the vicinity. The mother was there. Julienne breathed a sigh of relief; she was not alone. Several of the neighbors were with her, holding her hands, rubbing her shoulders. Julienne wished she knew something to say to the woman, but she could think of nothing. An invisible weight pressed on her chest as she struggled to do something appropriate, something helpful. But she could not help Colin and she could not help this woman. She was barely able to keep from screaming. It seemed like hours that she stood there, staring at the grieving group.

Colin came through the door. Julienne looked hopefully at him, but he was not looking for her. "Mrs. MacEnzie?"

The trembling woman looked up at him. "Yes?" She stood up to await the verdict.

"We think your son is going to be okay."

A general sigh of relief filled the room. "Thank the Lord."

"He's not out of the woods yet," Colin cautioned. "We've stopped the internal bleeding and set the broken bones, but he's still unconscious. We're not sure why."

As his words sunk in, the woman's face clouded over.

"The nurses are taking him to a room right now."

"But we have no money!" the woman cried.

"Mrs. MacEnzie, your son must stay in the hospital. I'll speak to the hospital administrator."

She nodded and, as she clutched her friend's hand, said, "May I see him?"

Colin nodded. "He's sleeping, but if you'd like to sit with him, you may."

"You go, Mary," one of the neighbors said. "I'll find Frank and send him over."

"Thank you." Mrs. MacEnzie nodded at her friend and looked again at Colin.

"Room 207." He softly answered her unasked question.

After a few more moments of quick planning, the crowd in the waiting room thinned out. Julienne was left face to face with Colin.

"Julienne, are you all right?"

She swallowed and replied, "Yes, yes, of course."

"You look very pale."

"Well, it's. . .I . . ." She looked into his gray eyes. "I didn't know what to do, Colin." She spoke flatly.

"You did what I asked you to do."

She shook her head. "No. I was too slow. I just stared at him, while you. . ."

"I did what I'm trained to do. You're only a first-year nursing student. Don't berate yourself over this."

Julienne reached out and gripped his arm. "Colin. Please . . .help me understand this."

He led her to a pair of upright wooden chairs and they sat down side by side. "Start at the beginning, Julienne," he said gently.

Gradually she released her grip on his arm and started to breathe more regularly. "I don't think I can do this, Colin."

"If you don't want to talk now, we can—"

"No, I mean medicine. I don't think I'm cut out for working in this field."

"Julienne, what you saw today was horrible. A small child falling from an open window and landing on the sidewalk. Your response is completely normal."

"But I shouldn't be normal. I'm in training to be a nurse. But I didn't know what to do, and I couldn't make myself move."

"You haven't spent much time in emergency situations. You won't always feel this way. Don't let one incident sidetrack you from something you've been working hard at."

"You don't understand, Colin. I've had doubts for a long time. All summer, really. The truth is that I came back more to get away from my mother than out of conviction or some sense of calling. I've been afraid it's all a pretense that would come crashing down. And now it has."

Colin was finally silent. The weight of her reaction had finally sunk in. "I'm sorry, Julienne. I had no idea."

"I couldn't tell you." She spoke in a whisper and could not look at his face. "You were so sure I should be here. I didn't want to disappoint you."

Impulsively, Colin wrapped his arms around her and hugged her to his chest. He had never done that before. Julienne was taken by surprise, but comforted.

"Julienne, you can't disappoint me by being true to yourself. I don't want you to be here to please me." He laughed lightly. "If you want to live your life to please someone else, you can go home to Maine and please your mother."

Julienne grimaced. "Never."

"I'm here because this is where God wants me to be and because I'm happy here. I believe I'm going to be happy being a pediatrician, despite things like what happened today." He cupped her chin and turned her face upward so that she had to look at him. "I know I suggested that you come to Chicago. And I still believe you'll make a wonderful nurse. You're smart and caring and gentle, just the way a nurse should be."

She drew back from him. "Colin, you are the only person in the world who sees those qualities in me. It sounds flattering, but I'm not sure it's true."

"Of course it's true."

She shook her head but he persisted.

"Julienne, look at me. You don't have to believe me any more than you believe your mother. You have to believe God."

"God?" she asked.

"Look, I'm not going to preach at you about this. But don't throw in the towel yet. Think about what I've said."

A nurse appeared next to them. They had not noticed her approach. "Dr. Covington," she said. "Dr. Reynolds is waiting for you in pediatrics. Will you be joining rounds?"

Colin looked from the nurse to Julienne and nodded. "Please tell him I'll be right up." He reached for Julienne's hand and gave it a squeeze. "I have to go. Maybe we can talk more on the weekend."

She nodded wordlessly as he stood up and left. She was calmer than she had been a few minutes earlier but was just as confused and she struggled to make sense of what Colin had said. Was it true that she was running away from her mother only to surrender to someone else's dream for her? By staying in Chicago, was she choosing the best of two undesirable alternatives? What was the point of staying in school if she did not believe she could ever be a nurse? And what did Colin see in her that she did not see in herself?

୨ଈ

It was late and the dormitory was still. Julie selected the "save" option from her computer screen and listened to the familiar whirring sounds as her English paper was stored in the hard drive. She was satisfied with what she had written that evening, though she might have a different opinion of it in the morning light. She still had another day to polish it up before it was due.

Though Julie had worked productively, Grammy was in the back of her mind all evening, along with the grandfather Julie had never known. She was the one grandchild born after his death. She had depended on picture albums and family memories to create an image of Colin Covington for her. On an impulse she pulled open the middle desk drawer and rummaged around for a small photo book. Opening it up, she lightly traced over the image of her grandparents on their wedding day. Grammy looked so young! In fact, she had been the age that Julie was now. Colin looked nervous but happy. Julie had never heard anything to lead her to believe that Julienne and Colin Covington had not been happy.

Julie wondered if it was possible to be lonely for someone she had never known. Maybe if she had known her grandfather she could understand Grammy better right now.

eight

"Julie, put that pad down and get in here," Marjorie insisted.

Julie rolled her eyes slightly but her pencil did not stop its swift, circular movements. Marjorie insisted on talking to Julie like she was one of her school-age daughters, but Julie refused to play the game. She would put her pad down when she was finished with the sketch. Grammy had fallen asleep sitting upright in the chair near the picture window in the living room. The waning afternoon light softened the woman's features with its gray hues and made an appealing image. Julie had done a lot of sketches of her grandmother in the last few weeks. She hoped to paint a portrait some day. In the meantime, she needed to practice drawing the old woman's face over and over, with different expressions and in different settings.

Marjorie appeared in the doorway. "I could really use some help in here. After all, it's your boyfriend who is coming to dinner."

I'm not the one who invited him, Julie thought to herself. She pressed her lips together to keep from speaking her thoughts. Aloud she said, "I'll be only another minute or two."

Marjorie seemed satisfied and disappeared into the kitchen. Julie did not understand why Marjorie was at their parents' home in the first place. Her mother had already planned the meal and Julie had come home in plenty of time to help if needed. But as soon as Marjorie heard that Liz Covington had invited Dennis to dinner, she had let it be known that she was planning to be there, too. In Julie's mind, that made the kitchen too crowded, so she had abdicated her culinary responsibilities in favor of sketching in the afternoon light.

Finally satisfied with her drawing, she set the pad down on the coffee table and reluctantly headed for the kitchen.

"Hi, Mom. What can I help with?"

Before Liz could answer, Marjorie said, "The table needs setting. Use the good china." She glanced at her younger sister's clothing. "Don't forget to leave yourself time to change."

"I'm not changing my clothes, Marjorie. You're making too big a deal over this. Do you want to use the white tablecloth, Mom?"

"That's fine, honey. Whatever you want."

"The blue one would be better," Marjorie said. "I picked up some new candles on my way over."

"Fine. I'll use the blue one."

"I think you should at least put on a fresh shirt."

Julie gripped the edge of the counter to keep from slamming her hand down on it. "Marjorie, it's nice of you to want to help out tonight, but I'm a big girl. I can decide whether I need to change my shirt or not."

Liz jumped in to divert the argument she knew was coming between her daughters. "Come on, Julie. I'll help you with the table."

Together they went through the doorway into the dining room. Julie pulled open a wide, deep drawer in the built-in china cabinet. Carefully pressed tablecloths were neatly stacked in the drawer. The blue one was on the bottom of the pile.

"Choose whatever tablecloth you want," her mother said, as if reading her mind.

Julie was tempted to take out the white one, on top of the stack, simply out of spite. With a sigh, she pulled out the blue one instead. "If we don't use the blue one, she'll give me dirty looks all night. It's not worth it."

"She means well." Liz opened a glass door and counted out six china plates with a delicate pastel floral pattern around the rim.

"Why isn't she home making dinner for her own family?"

"Steve is out of town and the girls are sleeping over at a friend's." Liz turned back to the cabinet for glasses. "Marjorie likes Dennis a lot, you know."

The tablecloth billowed in the air as Julie spread it over the table. "She thinks Dennis is highly marketable, that's all."

"Don't be silly."

"I'm not being silly, Mom. You know how she feels about my art. I'm sure she thinks that if I'm going to insist on pursuing it I ought to at least be married to someone who can provide financial security."

"Dennis has more to offer you than financial security," Liz said quietly as she counted out the silverware she needed.

Julie silently set the plates around the table. Her mother was right. Dennis had more to offer than a secure future. Even if he were not a computer whiz with three job offers, he would be crazy about Julie. And he never carped at her about her art. He would never stand in her way. Then again, he never really encouraged her art, either. It was part of who Julie was, and he accepted the whole package without picking apart individual elements. She was never sure how significant her painting was to Dennis.

"Just to humor your sister why don't we use cloth napkins?" Her mother's voice was lighthearted.

Julie gave a mock gasp of astonishment. "You were not seriously considering paper dinner napkins, were you? I'm sure there must be a special counseling program we could get you into so you can confront that problem."

Liz laughed. "They probably give shock treatment to people who put the salad fork on the wrong side of the plate."

Julie looked down at the handful of forks she held. "Don't tempt me." The door swung open just then.

"How's it going in here?" Marjorie asked authoritatively, a spatula in one hand.

Julie snapped to attention and saluted with her fistful of forks. "All utensils present and accounted for."

"Knock it off." Marjorie went back through the swinging door.

Julie and her mother looked at each other and burst out laughing.

&

Dennis arrived promptly at six o'clock with an assortment of carnations wrapped in florist's paper for Julie's mother. Liz took them gratefully and started for the kitchen in search of a vase.

"I think it will be a few more minutes until dinner," Julie said. "Let's sit down."

They sat side by side on the couch. Her grandmother still sat in the armchair across from them. "Tmm," she murmured. "Tmm fall."

"Does she need something?" Dennis asked quietly.

Julie shook her head. "She's thinking of something in the past, I suppose."

"Tmm. Tmm fall. Tom. Hurt."

"Is she calling your dad?"

Julie looked intently at her grandmother. "Maybe. I'll go get him."

She stepped across the entry hall to her father's study and returned with him in a moment. Tom Covington leaned over and took his mother's hand.

"Mom? Do you need something?" he asked gently.

She turned her head toward his voice. "Tom hurt?"

"No, Mom, I'm not hurt. I'm fine."

She looked away, her lips moving but no sound coming out.

Tom turned toward Julie and Dennis and shrugged.

Marjorie entered the room just then with a bright smile. "Hi, Dennis. It's so nice to see you."

Dennis rose and offered his hand in greeting. Marjorie shook it warmly.

"I didn't realize you were going to join us tonight," he said.

"My family all found better things to do tonight. Since I was on my own, I thought I'd come here."

"Well, it's nice to see you."

"I believe dinner is ready." Marjorie gestured toward the dining room.

Julie and her father helped Grammy out of her chair and she shuffled slowly to the dining room. Dennis pulled out her chair and they got her settled. Tom gave thanks for the meal.

Marjorie placed a platter of sliced roast beef in front of Dennis. "Go ahead, Dennis," she urged. "You're the guest of honor. You start."

Dennis seemed embarrassed but he obediently picked up the meat platter. "I don't know about being the guest of honor, but everything looks delicious." He passed the meat on to Julie and Marjorie handed him a bowl of mashed potatoes.

"Let's just say that we're celebrating your last semester of college."

"I won't argue with that." Tom took the meat from Julie and made his selection carefully.

"Will it be easier to get a job by graduating midyear?" Liz Covington asked. "Or do most companies wait till the spring to hire?"

Julie piped up, "Actually, Dennis has several job offers

already."

All heads turned toward Dennis.

"Oh?" said Tom and Liz together.

"Of course he does," said Marjorie. "Anybody would be a fool not to hire Dennis."

"The job market is difficult to break into these days," Liz said, as she cut meat and vegetables for her mother-in-law. "Congratulations, Dennis." She smiled at him affectionately.

"Thank you." He was embarrassed again.

"I never had any doubt Dennis would be able to get a job," Marjorie said. "After all, he took a very practical approach to his education. He's prepared for the business world."

Julie let her fork clank to her plate. Surely Marjorie was not going to get on her soapbox right then.

"I think it's wonderful, Dennis," Marjorie continued. "I'm sure whatever you choose, you and Julie will be in good shape.

Dennis turned to pass Julie the salad. She felt his eyes on her but purposely avoided them.

"So, tell us what the options are," Liz said.

Dennis launched into an enthusiastic description of all three jobs, the two in Chicago and the one in Seattle. Julie found herself smiling as she watched his animation. Clearly he was excited about his future. She was glad to see him so happy. With a stab of guilt, she had to honestly admit that she had been less than enthusiastic, maybe not even very interested in the decision he faced. Rationally she knew she ought to be interested; it could affect her life profoundly if she decided to marry him. But emotionally, she distanced herself from the whole process. Somehow marrying Dennis seemed like a college dream, and she did not know how to cope with the imminent reality.

The phone rang. Everyone remained absorbed in Dennis's explanations, so Julie popped up to answer it, grateful for the excuse to leave the table for a moment.

"Julie, is that you?" a voice said.

"Larry?"

"Hello. I called your dorm and they said you had gone home for the weekend."

"I usually do. I like to see my grandmother."

"How is she?"

"About the same. Worse maybe. We're moving her to a nursing home next weekend." She thought they had already made their plans and wondered why Larry was calling. "What's going on?"

"Well, I've had a slight change of plans. There's a seminar I really should go to next Wednesday. I know you said that would be a good day to get together, but I wonder if there is any possibility we could do it on Thursday."

"Thursday?" She pondered her schedule for the week of his visit. "I have classes in the morning, but I should be done for the day by about one o'clock."

"That would still give us most of the day. If that's all right with you, I think that would work better for me."

"It should be fine."

"Great. Then I'll call you from Chicago next week."

"I'll look forward to seeing you."

She hung up just as Marjorie came through the swinging door. "Who?" Marjorie asked, opening the refrigerator and removing a bottle of chilled water.

"What?"

"Look forward to seeing who?"

Julie shrugged. "Someone I met in Maine. He's coming to Chicago for a trade show."

"That carpenter guy?"

Julie did not like the condescending tone in her sister's voice. "He's not 'that carpenter guy.' His name is Larry Paxton and he's a friend. I'm entitled to have friends, aren't I?"

"Of course. What about Dennis?"

"What about him?"

"I just wonder what he thinks of this."

"Dennis has nothing to do with this." Julie's voice was rising.

"Whoa, take it easy, kid."

"Don't call me that."

"I've always called you that."

"Don't do it anymore."

Their mother peeked her head through the door. "Girls!" she whispered. "Must you quarrel right now?"

Julie fell silent and averted her eyes. "Let's just finish dinner."

Wordlessly they all returned to the dining room and took their seats. Julie picked up her fork and started moving food around on her plate. She had lost her appetite.

"You all right?" Dennis asked, his eyes quietly searching for a clue.

She smiled slightly and nodded. She was not sure how much of her outburst he had heard before her mother put a stop to it. Changing the subject, she said, "That was a friend from Maine. I think I told all of you about Della and Larry and the old house. He's coming to town next week for a convention and wants to see me."

"Hey, that's great," Dennis said in his usual good-natured way. "Will I get to meet him?"

Julie felt the blood drain from her face. She had not entertained the possiblity that Dennis and Larry would meet. There was no reason why they should not. "Depends what you're doing on Thursday afternoon," she said lightly.

"I have a full tutoring schedule on Thursday afternoons." He looked genuiney disappointed.

"Maybe something will work out," Julie said, though she doubted it. She was not sure she even wanted something to work out.

Julie had successfully diverted attention from her show of temper. The rest of the dinnertime conversation was casual, though Marjorie did not say much for the remainder of the meal. After the homemade cherry pie and freshly brewed coffee, Marjorie and Liz disappeared into the kitchen and Tom returned to his study. Julie and Dennis were once again alone with Grammy.

"Does she understand anything anymore?" Dennis asked quietly, his arm around Julie's shoulders as they sat on the couch. "When I first met you, she was already sick, but it seemed like she knew who I was."

"She did. But I don't know anymore. I'm not sure she knows any of us anymore." She leaned her head against his shoulder. "I'm worried what will happen to her once she's in the nursing home."

"She'll be well looked after, I'm sure."

Julie nodded silently. Wasn't her grandmother entitled to more than being looked after?

nine

Melanie was still asleep when Julie woke the next Saturday morning. Julie had tossed restlessly most of the night. When morning finally came, she was relieved. It was time to move Grammy. She took her clothes into the bathroom to dress without disturbing Melanie and then slipped out the front door of the dorm to wait for Dennis.

Dennis had insisted on coming along, and she was grateful. Julie was not sure of what to expect from the day; she was afraid she would be too worn out to drive home at the end of the afternoon.

It was late enough in September that the early morning sky was hazy gray and overcast. Although there was still hope for an Indian summer, a cold spell had settled in and the morning was especially brisk. Julie had layered her clothing against the chill in the air. Still she shivered. She plunged her hands deep into the pockets of her stadium jacket and looked hopefully down the road.

Dennis lived in a dorm on the other side of the campus, but he was always prompt. She was certain he would not leave her standing in the cold. Finally she saw his maroon sedan emerge from the shadows. He stopped in front of her and leaned over and threw open the door. Subdued, she sat down next to him and turned her face for an habitual kiss.

"Nervous?" he asked.

"Not exactly nervous. Apprehensive."

Dennis lifted an eyebrow and silently encouraged her to say more.

"I know in my brain that Grammy does not understand what's happening. It probably won't make any difference to her where she is. I just hate that it has come down to this."

With one hand he squeezed her fingers as he used the other hand to turn the steering wheel onto the main road out of the campus. "I don't know what to say, Julie. I know this is hard for you. But I'm glad you let me come along."

She reached out and stroked his forearm. "I'm glad you're coming." She truly was glad. Dennis had a compassionate side that shone in moments like this.

At her parents' house they filled the trunks of two cars with clothing, linens, and select personal items. As Julie and Dennis, Liz and Tom went back and forth with several loads, Julienne Leed Covington sat proudly erect in the living room, as if supervising the whole operation. Someone looking in the picture window from the outside would never know her true condition. But instead of following their motion back and forth across the room, in and out the door, her eyes were fixed straight ahead at the wall across from her chair. At last Tom led his mother gently to his car, buckled her in, and the convoy began. Jane and Fran would be waiting for them at Prairie Valley.

Julie checked her watch at the beginning and end of the trip. She wanted to know exactly how long it would take to get out to see Grammy on future visits. Eighteen minutes.

They parked their cars side by side in the guest parking area in front of the sprawling brick building. Slamming her door behind her, Julie took a moment to look at the structure spreading out in several directions. She knew that one end was an independent living wing, but Grammy could not stay there. At the other end was a section for residents needing serious health care. Eventually Grammy might go there. In the middle was the section where her grandmother would be for now: where the clients needed to be checked on often but did not have to be restricted to bed. It looked well kept, just as her aunts had said.

Julie stepped over to help her father get Grammy out of the backseat of his car. She looked confused as she emerged from the dim interior of the car into the daylight. She seemed to be struggling to recognize something. Julie and her father each took one elbow and steered her toward the front door. Liz and Dennis trailed behind.

Jane and Fran were already inside, filling out the paperwork. They hardly looked up when the entourage entered the lobby.

"Room 116," Jane said flatly, gesturing with the end of a ball point pen. "Down the hall and to the right."

"Good morning to you, too," Julie said, clearly irritated at her Aunt Jane's dispassionate welcome of her mother.

"Don't start with me," Jane warned, still not looking up from her stack of forms.

Liz shot Julie a look that reminded her of her promise to behave herself no matter what Jane and Fran did. Dennis put his hand on her shoulder, as if to rein her in.

Julie stepped away from Dennis and linked arms with her grandmother. "Let's go see your new room, Grammy," she said cheerily. She slowed her steps to meet the shuffling pace of the old woman.

Grammy stopped in her tracks, almost pulling Julie off balance.

"Grammy? What's wrong?" Julie asked.

Grammy's eyes were nearly closed to slits. Her lips began working. "Can't. No. Tom hurt."

"Tom is fine, Grammy. He's right here behind us." Gently she tried to urge her grandmother forward.

Grammy stopped again after one slow step. "No home.

Can't go. Tmmm."

Julie looked over her shoulder at her father, who only shrugged. He stepped forward to do what he could.

"Come on, Mom. There's a nice new room waiting for you. It has a big window and faces east. You'll be able to watch the sun rise in the mornings."

The old woman had frozen and would not budge.

"Would you like a wheelchair?" A nurse had observed their difficulty and stepped out from behind the registration desk.

Julie glanced at her father, who nodded and said, "Perhaps that would help."

They stood silently in the hall, Julie patting her grandmother's hand softly and steadily. The old woman continued to mutter but the sounds were unintelligible, even though Julie listened as closely as she could. Grammy never relaxed her stiff posture.

Jane and Fran had finished the paperwork and now leaned against the desk impatiently. Jane looked at her watch several times. It seemed like hours before an orderly arrived with a wheelchair.

Grammy had locked her knees, and getting her to sit down was no easy task. She kept shaking her head mournfully. Once she looked into Julie's eyes, and Julie thought she saw a flicker of recognition. Then it was gone. Finally they had her tucked into the chair. Tom started pushing it down the hall toward Room 116. The eyes of several residents sitting in the hallway followed their motion; some were more alert than others. They all seemed to slump in resignation to their condition. More than once Julie wanted to snatch her grandmother out of the wheelchair and whisk her out of the building. But she knew this had to be done.

Julie went ahead of her father. When she came to Room 116, she pushed open the wide door and looked around.

Trying not to let her disappointment show, she scanned the sparse room. The bed nearer to the door was already occupied with a woman nearly as old as her own grandmother. She looked pale and fragile; Julie found herself looking away.

"So you've brought me a new roommate," the woman said abruptly, in sharp, crisp rhythm. Julie was surprised at how clear and strong her voice was. It took a second for her to collect her thoughts and respond.

"Yes, my grandmother." She held the door open and her father wheeled Grammy in, followed by the rest of the group.

"Good. I've been lonely."

Julie was not sure whether she should tell the woman that her grandmother would not be much company or let her figure it out for herself. She said nothing.

The woman ignored her hesitation. "My name's Isabel Jackson. Who are you?"

Her bluntness took Julie by surprise. "Julie Covington." The woman seemed to want more. Julie gestured at the others. "These are my parents, my aunts, and my boyfriend."

"You'll be visiting?"

Julie glanced at the others, not wanting to speak for them. "I will, yes."

"Good."

Isabel seemed satisfied and turned away in her bed.

Tom and Liz were busy trying to transfer Grammy from the wheelchair to an armchair. Julie inspected the room.

In addition to the two beds, there were two worn looking vinyl armchairs on each side of a small table in front of the window. Each bed had a nightstand and the bathroom was nearby. There was not much else. The walls were a putty gray color with no warmth and no adornment. The window had a venetian blind but no curtains. It did face east but looked out over a parking lot and a barbed wire fence.

It bothered Julie that there was no color in the room and she vowed to do something about that. She could do nothing about the view.

Grammy seemed settled. Her bottom lip was pushing in and out rapidly but she remained calm.

Tom turned to Dennis. "Why don't you help me with her things, Dennis? Julie can sit with her a while."

"Sure." Dennis was ready to help however he could.

"Then I guess you don't need us any longer," Fran said.

Tom looked surprised. "Well. . .I thought. . .till she was settled."

"You have to let go, Tom."

"We just got here, Fran."

"I can't believe you would just dump her like this!" Julie's voice rose to a shout rapidly.

"Shhh," said Jane, glancing at Mrs. Jackson.

"Don't shush me!"

"We are not 'dumping' her, as you so indelicately put it." Jane kept her voice low and made her point quickly. "We've made sure all the papers are in order, taken care of the financial arrangements, and so forth."

"She doesn't even have her coat off yet!"

Fran darted a fierce look at her brother. "Tom, do something with this child."

Julie was sorry to have involved her father in this. To her surprise, he defended her.

"She's not a child. She's a grown woman who loves her grandmother. She's just speaking her mind."

Clearly Fran had not expected such a response, either.

Jane was irate now. "I will not tolerate this continued disparaging of our efforts to look after Mother."

"Please, Jane," Liz said quietly. She threw a warning glance at Julie, too.

Jane ignored her sister-in-law. "If your daughter can speak her mind, so can I. She's been continually ungrateful about any attempt I've made to deal with this situation and I don't want to hear it anymore."

Julie felt Dennis's hand on the small of her back, pressing her forward. She knew she should say something to diffuse the tension.

"I'm sorry, Aunt Jane," she finally said, barely audible. "I do appreciate your making the arrangements. This looks like a nice place."

Jane sighed heavily. "I'm sure you don't mean a word of that, but I suppose it's all I'll get."

Julie's head snapped up, ready for the fight. Dennis grabbed her hand and wordlessly restrained her.

"Come on, Dennis," Tom said. "Let's get her things."

The room emptied out. Jane and Fran would not be back, Julie was certain of that. She turned to her grandmother.

"Well, Grammy, let's get your coat off. It's plenty warm in here." Shedding her own jacket and tossing it on the bed, Julie reached out to unbutton her grandmother's coat.

"You always speak out like that?" Isabel asked.

Isabel had been so quiet and still that Julie had nearly forgotten her presence. Suddenly embarrassed about her behavior, she flushed.

"Sorry about that," she muttered.

"Nothing to be sorry about. Who was that crabby old woman?"

Julie could not help but laugh. "My Aunt Jane. She made all the arrangements to bring my grandmother here."

"And you don't like it one bit."

Julie had to be truthful. "No, not really. But it's necessary." Gently she pulled her grandmother's arms out of her coat.

"Not such a bad place, you know. Checked myself in three

years ago. My son wanted me to live with him, but I wouldn't. He up and had a heart attack and died anyway."

As Julie hung the coat in the closet, she sized up the frail woman in the bed. Obviously, her mind was clear. The energy in her words overshadowed failures in her body.

"I'm sorry about your son."

"No need."

"I'm afraid my grandmother won't be much company for you. She has Alzheimer's."

Isabel shrugged. "No matter. Still nice to have someone to talk at, even if she doesn't talk back." She gave a high-pitched laugh. "Maybe it's even better that way."

Julie smiled and nodded.

Dennis returned with a suitcase and a cardboard box. Her parents soon followed. They spent the rest of the morning hanging clothes and putting linens away. Someone would have to come once a week and take the laundry to wash. Julie was sure it would not be Fran or Jane. Although her grandmother seemed unaware of the gesture, Julie set a picture of her grandparents, taken more than thirty years ago, on the nightstand next to Grammy's bed.

"Do they allow pictures on the wall?" Julie asked anyone who might be able to answer.

"Need permission for a nail," Isabel said in clipped tones, "but it can be done."

Julie pressed her lips together, satisfied. "Good. I'll bring in some pictures if you don't mind."

"Don't matter to me."

It would not matter to her grandmother, either, but Julie wanted to do it.

"Eleven-thirty. Lunchtime," Isabel informed the group. "I'll show you to the lunch room."

To Julie's surprise, the woman sat up and swung her legs

over the side of the bed. She was dressed in a housecoat and
slid her feet into slippers.

"Did you think I couldn't walk?" Isabel said, at Julie's surprised expression.

"Well. . .I. . .I didn't know."

"Never mind, missy. Just follow me."

As she guided her grandmother down the hall, Julie felt
strangely comforted by Isabel's confident presence. Maybe
Prairie Valley would work out after all.

ten

Larry was one of the first passengers off the train. Julie had been strangely nervous all morning, hardly able to concentrate on her classes. Now she stood on the platform watching him stride toward her with a pleasant, friendly smile on his lips. Julie almost did not recognize him; he had grown a dark, full beard in the two months since she had seen him. She smiled back at him and started to move toward him. But she was still nervous.

Illinois was the wrong context for Larry Paxton. He belonged far away, in Maine, wearing grubby clothes and working on a messy job. For Julie, he represented a short, pleasurable phase where she had indulged herself for ten weeks of intensive painting and made some new friends along the way. While indulging herself, she had also embarrassed herself by allowing Larry to see that she was attracted to him. She had somehow managed to put the incident behind her at the time, largely by leaving Maine a few days later. She had not expected to see Larry any time soon, and certainly not on her own territory.

But there he was, his dark hair and beard glimmering in the midday sun. Dressed in gray slacks and a blue jacket, he looked more like the corporate accountant that he had once been than the do-it-yourself remodeler that he now was. Julie was staring, she suddenly realized, and forced herself to move her eyes.

He had a package under his arm, which he extended to her. "Mom would not let me come empty-handed," he said.

She took the package. "Something homemade?"

"Of course."

They started walking toward the parking lot.

"It's so strange to see you here," Julie said.

"I admit I feel a little out of my element."

"You look great!" She had not meant to sound so enthusiastic and decided to change the subject quickly. "How is the trade show going?"

His eyes lit up. "Great! I'm learning a lot. Mom ran that little motel in New Jersey before we bought Leed House, but owning our own business is a different matter. We haven't even begun to think about promotion once we get the place ready to open, or what special guest services we want to offer. Even the price we set will communicate something about our quality."

Julie laughed. "I thought you and Della were looking for the simple life."

He cocked his head playfully. "We are. But we have to make a living, you know. You might pay just for the pleasure of staring at Leed House, but no one else will."

"I don't need to stare at it anymore," Julie retorted. "I have over forty sketches of it. I've got every inch of it memorized."

"Ah, but that's the old Leed House. You have not yet seen the full transformation."

"True," she conceded.

"Mom wants to know when you're coming back out."

"I hadn't thought that far ahead. If I don't get tied down to some job after graduation. . ." She left the sentence unfinished. Or if I don't get tied down to Dennis, she thought.

They reached her car and she unlocked the doors.

"I hope you've picked a nice restaurant," Larry said. "Mom's instructions are to give you the royal treatment."

"Well, I'm not sure what she had in mind, but I'll do my

best to have a good time."

As she pulled out of the parking lot and headed toward the restaurant, Julie realized that she felt more relaxed than a few minutes ago. She had purposely selected a place where she and Dennis had never been together before. It was a modest place with a casual setting, where she would feel comfortable.

"I hope you like Italian food," she said lightly.

"Of course. Been eating it all my life. My mother's one of the best Italian cooks I know."

"You mean your mother is Italian?"

"Didn't you know?"

"I guess I never realized it. But it makes sense. Paxton doesn't sound Italian, but of course that's her married name." She turned into the restaurant's parking lot. "Well, then, I hope this place is up to your usual standards."

They had a surprisingly pleasant meal together. Julie recovered from her earlier nervousness and her anxiety over what they would talk about all afternoon disappeared in a steady stream of conversation. Most of what they chatted about had to do with what was going on at Leed House or in Seabridge, Maine, since that is what they had in common. Larry had hired a contractor to put in private bathrooms in each of the guestrooms. Della was busy wallpapering the downstairs rooms and rummaging around the county looking for furniture that would suit the Victorian decor she hoped to create. In the spring, when the weather cleared up again, Larry would arrange to have the outside painted. They would miss the summer season, but they should be ready for the tourists who came to see the fall colors. Julie had left behind one painting of Leed House and Della wanted to hang it prominently in the main parlor to welcome their guests.

Julie reported on moving her grandmother into the nursing

home and the family tensions that remained unresolved. Even as she spoke, she heard the bitter edge in her own voice but she could not stop it.

"Do you think she's going to be happy there?" Larry asked.

Julie shrugged and pushed out her bottom lip. "Who can say? We really don't know what she's feeling most of the time."

"Well, then, are you satisfied that it's the right place for her?"

"That's not really up to me to decide. But I suppose so."

"Have you been to see how she's doing?"

Julie shook her head. "I was hoping to go on the weekend."

"Let's go today."

She stared at him and her mouth dropped open. "You want to go see my grandmother?"

"Sure. Why not?"

"She won't know we're there."

"Doesn't matter."

"But there must be dozens of things more interesting for you to see on a visit to Illinois."

"I'm not visiting Illinois. I'm visiting you. I know how important your grandmother is to you. Otherwise you would never have come to Maine hunting for her childhood home."

"Well, yes, but there's no reason that you—"

"Then we'll go. I'll get the check."

❧

Julie was still in shock when they arrived at Prairie Valley Nursing Center about forty minutes later. She signed in on the visitors list at the main desk and then led the way down to Room 116. Her grandmother sat in one of the chairs by the window. Isabel Jackson sat in the other.

"Who's this?" Isabel demanded, looking at Larry.

"A friend."

"This is not the young man you had here the other day."

Julie blushed and said, "That was Dennis. This is Larry. I met him last summer in Maine."

"Good. You're young. It's good to have more than one young man at your age."

"Oh, no, I don't—"

Larry smiled and shook his head slightly, letting her know that further explanations were not necessary for his sake.

"It's nice to see you, Mrs. Jackson," Julie said as she took her grandmother's hand. She knelt in front of her and searched for a visual connection.

"Grammy? Are you all right?"

The old woman's eyes darted around without settling on anything.

"I brought someone to meet you. He's from Maine. He lives at Leed House now."

"Leed," Grammy muttered.

"Yes, Leed House. He's fixing it up really nice. You'd like it."

Larry sat on the edge of the bed, squarely in front of Julie's grandmother. "I'm happy to meet you, Mrs. Covington. Julie has told me a lot about you."

Her eyes seemed to settle on Larry. She reached up and grazed his beard with her fingertips. "Leed. . .Lor. . .gone."

"I think she's really looking at you," Julie whispered.

Larry shrugged and smiled.

"No home." The flicker of recognition was gone. Grammy started pushing her bottom lip in and out, but she said nothing more.

"Maybe she'd like to take a little walk down the hall or something," Larry suggested.

"That's a good idea." She turned to Isabel. "You won't mind if we steal her away for a few minutes, will you?"

"Not time for her walk."

"What do you mean?"

"We walk in the morning. Ten o'clock."

"Well, I think it would be all right if we took her again."

"Suit yourself."

"Come on, Grammy." Julie gently urged her grandmother to her feet. Larry took the other elbow. Together the three of them shuffled across the room and out the door. They walked for twenty minutes or so and then brought Grammy back to her room. She seemed to stare at Larry again. Before they left, she whispered, "Lor gone." Julie made sure she was settled again and kissed her grandmother goodbye.

As they left Prairie Valley, Julie said, "I promised my parents I'd bring you by the house. I hope you don't mind."

"Not at all. I'd like to meet them."

"I feel like I'm dragging you around to all the mundane corners of my life instead of letting you do something fun."

"Hey, I left the rat race on purpose, remember? It's the quiet life for me now."

Julie looked over at him and smiled. "Good. Dad is especially interested in hearing more about the house."

"Has he ever seen it?"

She shook her head. "Grammy never went back, from what I can tell."

"I'll try to make it sound exciting."

"Mom will probably want to feed you."

"Are all mothers like that? I thought mine was the only one."

"Well, yours is a champion, that's for sure."

A few minutes later they pulled into the driveway of the Covington house. Julie led the way in through the back door.

"Mom? Are you here?"

"In here." Her voice came from the dining room. Julie

pushed open the swinging door and saw her mother at the table with papers spread all around her.

"Just catching up on the bills," Liz said, not looking up.

"Mom, I'd like you to meet someone."

Liz looked up. "You must be Larry." She stood up and extended her hand. "It's so nice to meet you. Julie was quite smitten with Leed House."

"It's hard not to fall in love with that old place," Larry said.

"I hope you'll stay for dinner."

Larry and Julie smiled at each other knowingly. "My pleasure," he answered.

"My husband should be home soon. I'll get things started. Julie, why don't you show Larry around for a while?"

Liz disappeared into the kitchen and they heard her extracting pots and pans from the cupboard.

"This is a nice house," Larry said, glancing around. "Homey."

"I've lived here all my life, except for being in the dorm at school." She gestured toward the next room. "I'll show you around."

The tour ended in a room at the back of the garage that Julie often painted in. During high school her father had added better lighting and permanently surrendered the space to her interests. She snapped on the light switch as they came through the door. Light flooded the dim room, revealing stacks of canvases and two easels.

Larry looked at her, surprised. "I never knew you had a studio!"

Julie waved away the thought. "It's not really a studio. Just an extra room that I'm lucky enough to be able to use."

"From the looks of things, you spend a lot of time here."

"Well, some of these paintings go back seven or eight years.

They're not very good. A childish effort."

"Some day when you are a famous artist, they'll be worth something."

She gave a short laugh. "That will never happen."

"Why not?"

"I'm not that good."

"Don't put yourself down. May I?" He gestured toward a stack of canvases leaning against one wall.

"Sure. But don't get your hopes up. And don't say anything just to be nice."

Larry slowly flipped through the paintings, studying each one carefully before going to the next one. There were portraits of people of various ages. He recognized two portraits of her parents. The landscapes ranged from ducks on a lake to a farm in a winter blizzard. What surprised him most were the abstract expressionistic paintings with splotches of color placed in a seemingly random way but with a mysterious sense of order.

"Wow. This is impressive."

"You don't have to say that."

He looked up at her. "But I really mean it. I had no idea."

"You watched me paint all summer."

"But all you ever painted was Leed House. I had no idea you were so versatile."

"I've tried a lot of different styles. That doesn't mean that I'm good at any of them."

"But you are! The way you capture light. . .it's as if something is struggling to shine through whatever you paint; there's a sort of glow that comes through all the different styles."

Julie was getting embarrassed. "Like I said, some of those are really old. I don't think I've really developed a style of my own yet."

"I hope that you came home from Maine with the conviction that you should be an artist."

Julie hedged against such a bold statement. "Well, I know that I want to be in the art field in some capacity."

"I'd hate to see you drawing greeting card covers."

"It would be a way to make a living."

"I'm no art critic, but I think you could make some money off of some of these paintings. Have you ever thought about selling them?"

Julie felt the color drain from her face. "It never occurred to me that anyone would want them."

"I do."

"You do what?"

"I want some of the paintings."

"Well, I could give you one, I suppose."

"No, Julie, I don't want you to give me one. I want to buy one."

"You're not serious."

He nodded adamantly. "I am indeed serious." He pulled out one canvas. "This winter scene, for instance, would look great in the house. It could be Maine."

"It's Michigan."

"Well, we get blizzards like that in Maine. The light coming from the little farmhouse makes the whole painting feel warm, in spite of the snow."

"Larry, I don't know. . ."

"Julie, you never will be an artist if you don't show people your work."

"But I'm not ready for that. I'm not good enough."

"Please let me buy this painting."

He looked into her blue eyes with his brown ones. She studied his face as subtly as she could. He was sincere. He really wanted her painting.

"Okay, I guess," she finally mumbled.

"Will I be pressing my luck to ask for two?"

She looked at him with wide eyes. "Two?"

He nodded.

Julie was relieved to hear her mother calling them for dinner. Eating would give her an excuse not to talk for a while—and a chance to absorb what had just happened. No one had ever been this interested in her paintings before, not even Dennis. For the first time in her life, she had met someone who genuinely believed she could be an artist. It was enough to make her start believing it herself.

Larry lingered at the Covington house much longer than anyone intended. Finally, he and Julie had to rush out the door so he could catch the last train back to Chicago for the night. They nearly trotted to the platform where the train was already warming up.

"Guess I'd better get on, " Larry said. He stopped in front of the third car and faced her.

"It looks ready to go. Tell your mom I said hello."

"I'll do that." He paused awkwardly and then unexpectedly leaned down and kissed her cheek.

"Goodbye, Julie." The whistle blew and he moved toward the train.

"Goodbye." Her voice was just a whisper as she watched him disappear into the car.

eleven

"Julienne!" someone called.

She lifted her groggy head from the pillow. Had she heard someone call her name? A soft knock on her door confirmed that someone was looking for her.

"Julienne," the voice said in a harsh whisper. "Wake up." The knocking grew insistent.

Julienne turned on the light at her bedside and looked at the clock. It was after one o'clock in the morning.

The voice outside her locked door was growing impatient. "It's the middle of the night. Open up!"

Julienne put on her housecoat and winced as her bare feet hit the cold wood floor. She tiptoed across the room, shivering. When she opened the door, she saw an irritated Mrs. Davis glaring at her.

"You have a phone call."

"At this hour?"

Mrs. Davis scowled, obviously insulted that Julienne would doubt her.

"I'm sorry your sleep was disturbed, Mrs. Davis." A phone call in the middle of the night could only be bad news. She scurried down the stairs in her bare feet.

"Hello?"

"It's me." It was Colin's voice.

"Is it Thomas?" she asked urgently. She could think of no other reason he would call in the middle of the night.

"Yes. He's not doing well."

"Oh, no! Will he—"

Colin cut off her worst fears. "We just don't know. If you want to see him, I'll come for you."

"No! You stay with him. I'll be there as soon as I can."

She hung up the phone and turned to go back up the stairs to dress.

"Where do you think you're going in the middle of the night?"

Julienne, thinking that her housemother had gone back to bed, was surprised to see her standing at the foot of the stairs.

"To the hospital. There's an emergency."

"But you're not qualified to help."

Julienne was getting annoyed at the delay. "Not medically. But I can be there. There are other ways to help a sick child."

Mrs. Davis softened. "The little boy who fell?"

Julienne nodded.

"Go," said the housemother. "But remember you have classes in the morning."

"I won't miss them," Julienne promised as she went flying up the stairs.

In the two weeks since she and Colin had seen Thomas fall from his apartment window, Julienne had followed the boy's case closely. Colin had missed two nights of sleep in a row trying to keep Thomas stable. He insisted that Julienne keep up with her school schedule and rest properly, but he did not allow himself the luxury of more than a twenty-minute nap. Thomas and his parents were complete strangers to her but somehow the fact that she had witnessed his fall bound her to them. She had not been able to turn her back and walk away, unaffected by what she had seen. It was difficult to study. In between classes she climbed the stairs to the pediatric wing to check on Thomas.

After a four-day coma, Thomas regained consciousness. Julienne was in the room, watching him sleep, when he first stirred and asked for his mother. Waking up was a good sign, but the internal injuries were more severe than Colin had thought at first, and the boy struggled every day to take another step toward recovery. His lungs had filled with fluid and his leg bone would not set properly. There had been one complication after another.

Thomas's parents did not say much. His father, Frank, worked long hours in a meat packing plant and had been to the hospital only a few times. Mary, his mother, came every day and stayed with him as much as she could, but she had four other children to look after. Julienne never knew what to say to the crumpled, despairing woman, but she was no longer afraid of the silence of grief. She simply sat with Mary, not speaking much, and checked on Thomas as much as she could between classes and in the evening. She even studied there while he slept, watching the clock so she could slip into the dorm just before curfew.

The boy recognized her during his short periods of wakefulness. He found her name difficult to say and called her "Juwen." The moment he had first called her by name was when she lost her heart to him.

Now, bundled up against the night chill, Julienne hurried down the dimly lit street toward the hospital. She went through the main entrance and headed down the hall toward the stairs.

"Excuse me, miss," said a stern voice behind her.

Julienne turned around. She did not recognize the guardian of the passageway, but she was seldom in the hospital at night and didn't know the night staff.

"May I help you?" Apparently the woman did not know Julienne either.

"I'm here to see a patient," Julienne said.

"Visiting hours are from nine to eleven o'clock in the morning and six to eight in the evening."

"Oh, I'm not a visitor. I'm a student nurse here."

The woman shook her head. "No visitors." She planted herself in Julienne's path.

"Please, you have to let me through. It's an emergency."

"Is it a family member?"

"No, but—"

"I'd suggest you come back in the morning."

Julienne was flushed from her dash from the dorm and she was quickly losing patience with this woman. She sighed and tried again.

"Dr. Covington is expecting me."

"Dr. Covington?"

"Yes. He's one of the interns."

"I know who he is."

"He's waiting for me right now. Call up to pediatrics and find out for yourself."

"Perhaps I will." She turned back to her desk in the hall.

As soon as the woman's back was turned, Julienne dashed down the hall.

"Miss! Miss!"

Julienne ignored the enraged voice behind her and pushed through the door to the stairs. She took them two at a time.

Colin met her with half a smile. He was just putting down the phone. "There is one very unhappy nurse downstairs."

"Never mind her. How's Thomas?"

"You can see for yourself." Colin pushed open the door to Thomas's room and let Julienne in.

The child was pale, his skin almost translucent. His thin chest rose and fell rapidly in quick, shallow breaths. He looked very small in the big hospital bed.

"He's got a high fever that we haven't been able to break," Colin said. "There must be an infection, but we're not sure what it is yet."

"Isn't there anything else you can do?" Julienne asked urgently, turning to look into Colin's haggard face. "Is there anything I can do?"

He looked quietly and deeply into her eyes. "His mother is coming in," he said. "Can you sit with her?"

Julienne choked back her tears and nodded.

"I'm going to go check on the results of the last test. Will you wait here for her?"

"Yes," she mumbled, sinking into a wooden chair.

Colin left and Julienne sat there stiffly, watching Thomas. Already small, he had lost weight during his two weeks in the hospital. His curly blond hair looked almost angelic against the pillow, but his face was far from peaceful. Even in his sleep his young face furrowed and strained against his illness.

Julienne put her head down in her hands and said aloud, "Why, God? Why this?"

The door creaked open and Mary MacEnzie appeared. She looked worse than Julienne had ever seen her, frazzled, disheveled, and distraught. Julienne wondered when the last time was that Mary had slept.

She pulled herself to her feet and went over and put an arm around Mary's shoulder, guiding the mother to the chair she had just vacated.

"I can't stay long," Mary said, struggling to keep her tone even. "The baby's sick and Frank needs to sleep so he can work in the morning."

What about you? Julienne wanted to cry out. But she did not. Mary was coping the best she knew how, and Julienne did not want to upset her equilibrium.

"Dr. Covington will be back in a few minutes." Julienne offered what little she knew as comfort to her tired companion.

"How long have you been here?"

"Only a few minutes."

"I don't know why you sit with him like you do, but it makes me feel better knowing someone is checking on him."

"I'm happy to do it. I wish I could do more."

"I can never thank you and the doctor enough. If you hadn't been there when he fell—" She stifled a sob.

Julienne remembered her own immobility on the day of the accident. She was not proud of the way she had reacted.

"Dr. Covington is the one who knew what to do," Julienne said.

Mary stood up and laid her hand against her son's cheek. "He's burning up."

Julienne nodded. "They're trying to get his fever down."

Mary sat on the end of the bed, her gaze fixed on her little boy. Julienne returned to the wooden chair. Her heart went out to Mary, as it did every time she saw her. They sat like that for perhaps twenty minutes, occasionally speaking softly to each other.

Mary pulled a tissue out of her coat pocket and wiped her nose. "I hate to leave him, but I have to go. If he doesn't make it, I don't—"

"That hasn't happened yet. Dr. Covington is not giving up."

Sniffling, the mother nodded. "I know I won't sleep all night. Tell him to call me if. . ."

"If there is any change, we'll call."

"I have to go look after the baby. Thomas is in the good Lord's hands now."

Julienne nodded and swallowed the lump in her throat. Soon after Mary left, the night nurse came in to check on Thomas.

"He's soaked his bedding trying to sweat off that fever," the nurse said. "I'll change it. Why don't you take a break?"

"I'll help you."

"I can manage. You go on."

Spurred on by the nurse, Julienne stepped out into the hall. The night shift nurses were busy with their routines, taking care of a whole floor full of sick children. Julienne looked around numbly, not sure where to go. Without ever consciously deciding to do so, she slowly walked toward the small chapel at the end of the floor. She had been there only once before, for a short service at the beginning of her training.

It was dark. The simple table in the front of the room held a small gold cross that glinted in the dim light filtering in from the hall. She did not turn on the lights, but simply sat down in a back pew and stared at that strange light shining against all odds through the darkness.

The silence brought her no comfort. The absence of any distracting sound made the questions ringing in her head multiply and echo menacingly. She closed her eyes and tried to pray; she was in a chapel, so she should try to pray. But she could not. It had been too long since she had wanted to pray. The little church in Seabridge, Maine, had not taught her how to find God in tragedy. She was not sure He was there.

"Why?" she said aloud. "Why, God? You have to save Thomas. You can't let him die."

"Julienne?"

The voice was hardly above a whisper, but she recognized it as Colin's. Surprised, she looked toward the voice and saw him standing against one of the side walls, silhouetted by the moonlight coming through the window.

"Colin. I didn't see you. I thought you had gone down to the lab."

"I did. I wanted to stop here for a minute, too."

"Do you come here often?"

He moved toward her, shadowlike. "Fairly often, especially when I'm in the hospital at night."

"Do you pray?"

"Sometimes." He sat beside her in the pew.

She shook her head. "But what's the point? I'm not sure God really cares anyway."

"What do you mean? Of course He cares."

"How can you be so sure? After all, He hasn't done anything for Thomas in the last two weeks. And the whole MacEnzie family. . .they have such a hard life. If God is love like everyone says, then why is this happening?"

Colin didn't answer right away. The tormenting question hung in the air between them.

"That's a major theological question, Julienne."

"I don't want theology, Colin. This is real life. There's a little boy down the hall who might not make it."

"I know. But things are not as cut and dried as you're trying to make them. Don't throw away God just because life is not perfect." He said no more. Colin was not the sort to preach. He simply said what he thought and let his words have their own effect.

Colin reached out in the dark and took her hand in his. "Let's go see how he is."

As soon as they stepped out into the hall, a nurse called out to them. "Dr. Covington, they want you in Thomas MacEnzie's room."

With a glance at each other they nearly ran down the hall, back to his room. If Thomas had taken another turn for the worse, the end might be near. Colin anxiously pushed open the door, with Julienne right behind him.

The nurse who had stayed to change his sheets was smiling. "I think the fever is breaking, Doctor." She put her hand on Thomas's face. "He feels cooler, and he opened his eyes a few minutes ago."

"Did he say anything?"

"No, but he seemed to recognize me."

Julienne gave an enormous sigh of relief. Just then the boy stirred.

"Juwen?"

She quickly stepped to the bedside and took his hand. "I'm here, Thomas."

"I don't feel so good."

Despite his complaint, Julienne could not help smiling. "But you will. Soon. You're really much better."

"Where's my mom?"

"She had to go home for a while. But she's coming back in the morning."

"That's okay. You're here." He turned his head toward her and smiled weakly.

"That's right. I'm here."

"I'm hungry."

Julienne looked up at Colin, with a silent question about whether Thomas could have food.

Colin was grinning widely. "Then we'll get you something to eat. Right away." Taking his cue, the nurse left to arrange a tray of food. Colin continued, "After that, you need to get some more sleep so you'll be wide awake for your mother in the morning."

Julienne caught Colin's eye through the tears in her own. As if reading her thoughts, he said quietly, "I think he'll be okay."

With the crisis past, Julienne looked at Colin thoroughly for the first time that night. Clearly he had not slept in a very long time. He rubbed the back of his neck and yawned.

"Go get some sleep," she said. "I'll stay with him."

Tucking one leg under the other, she settled on the edge of the bed. Colin said good night and left. Julienne looked at Thomas, who looked back at her with his eyes more clear and alert than she had ever seen them. Had God heard her feeble prayer? Or was Thomas's recovery merely a coincidence?

twelve

"Is that gravy thickening?" Marjorie looked over Julie's shoulder to check on the progress of the Thanksgiving meal.

"I don't know why you gave me this job," Julie complained. "You know I never get the lumps out."

"Then it's time you learned. Use a brisker motion when you stir."

Their mother whizzed into the room. "Did anyone put the rolls in the oven?"

"The turkey is cooling and the rolls are baking," Marjorie said confidently. As usual, she had everything under control.

"Well, the table is ready," Liz said, donning an apron. "What still needs to be done in here?"

Marjorie waved her hand toward the stove. "Potatoes need mashing."

The door swung open again. It was one of Marjorie's daughters. "This is boring," she wailed. "I can't even watch TV. Uncle Ted won't turn the channel."

"What's he watching?" Julie asked, still struggling with the gravy.

"Football! I hate football, but all those guys want to do is watch football. Dennis, too."

"Dinner will be ready in just a few minutes," Marjorie assured her. "Why don't you and your sister find something else to do for a little while."

"Like what?"

Julie interjected, "Go sit with Grammy. I'll bet she isn't watching the football game."

"Aunt Julie, Grammy doesn't do anything," the child moaned.

"Julie has a good idea." Marjorie surprised Julie by agreeing with her. "Go see Grammy. Help her come to the table and find her chair."

With a disgruntled groan, the girl left. But the door opened again.

"Any more pretzels?" asked Ted, setting an empty snack bowl on the cluttered kitchen table.

"No more pretzels," Marjorie said. "Dinner's almost ready."

Ted stepped to the stove and began lifting lids. "What all have we got?"

"What we have is enough people in the kitchen," Marjorie said sternly. "Out."

Ted stuck his finger in a bowl of freshly whipped cream. Marjorie slapped his hand.

"Okay, okay, I'm leaving."

Liz picked up a small tray of relishes and handed it to her son. "I think we could start putting things on the table."

"I get the message."

When everything was on the table, the Lovellton branch of the Covington clan gathered around the dining room table, with Dennis as a special guest. Julie sat next to him, with her grandmother on her other side and Ted next to Grammy. Marjorie and her family filled the other side of the table. Tom Covington waited ceremonially, carving knife in hand, for his wife to come through the door with the turkey. The twenty-two-pound bird was roasted to a perfect golden hue. Its aroma had filled the air for hours, a promise of culinary pleasure. Liz Covington was famous throughout the extended family for her tender Thanksgiving turkeys.

Julie surveyed the table, truly grateful for the traditional family gathering. Marjorie had not once nagged her about marketable job skills, so the day was unscarred. Ted had volunteered to pick up Grammy and bring her home for the day. This was the second year that Dennis had joined her family for Thanksgiving, and she was glad he was here.

The only hint of discouragement was knowing that Grammy, though she was thoughtfully included, probably was too unaware to appreciate four generations of the family gathered around one table. And at her age, it might be the last year that such an assembly happened. Grammy seemed quite compliant today, but distant. In between her kitchen duties, Julie had checked on Grammy frequently, but the response was always the same. There had not been a moment all day that Julie felt any sense of connection with her grandmother. Forlornly, Julie remembered that not so long ago Grammy would have been in the thick of the kitchen activity, probably making her famous rice pudding with raisins.

Julie's wandering thoughts were interrupted by her father's voice.

"Ah, that looks wonderful," Tom said as the steaming bird was placed before him. He waited as Liz took her seat at the other end of the table. "Let's pray."

Julie took her grandmother's hand and reached for Dennis's, too. As he gave her fingers an extra squeeze, she bowed her head.

"Heavenly Father, with our table full of the bounty You provide, we come humbly into Your presence," Tom intoned. "What we do on this one day each year is but a token of the gratitude we owe You. As we fill our physical bodies with this food and are mindful of what You have provided, make us also mindful of our need for spiritual food. Cause us to turn to You for that also. Remind us of our total dependence on You for each step of our lives, for the provision of every need, for the answer to every question. As we silently now thank You for Your presence in our lives, come upon us in a fresh way."

The moment of silence in the Thanksgiving prayer was a longstanding Covington tradition. Julie was not sure when it had started; they had done it as far back as she remembered.

Her father's words pricked her heart. Her life was full of question marks right now. Did God have the answers?

"It is in Your name that we pray," Tom concluded. "Amen."

"I want a roll," one of the girls said immediately. "I don't have to eat sweet potatoes, do I?"

Marjorie sighed. "No, you may have mashed potatoes. Watch Grandpa carve the turkey."

The Thanksgiving meal was underway. They ate richly of an abundance of traditional food. Forks clinked steadily against china; conversation was lighthearted; slowly but surely the mounds of food disappeared. Julie hardly thought it possible that their group of ten could consume what had been put on the table, but they came very close to finishing off everything but the turkey itself. Ted had been snacking all day, but that never affected his appetite. The rest of them had waited patiently for this midafternoon indulgence.

"Shall we have pie now?" Liz said as she began collecting plates to scrape.

Julie held back a burp. She could not possibly eat pie right then. "Maybe we should wait a while, Mom." She glanced around the table and found general agreement.

"Well, we've had the feast," Dennis said. "Now we pay the price." He pushed his chair back and picked up two empty serving bowls.

Marjorie smiled. "Nice to see you acting like one of the family."

"I've spent enough holidays here to know the routine," he

answered. "But I don't know where things go, so I'd better wash and let someone else put things away."

Cleaning up was a big job. Marjorie made Dennis wear a calico apron to protect his new sweater. He protested briefly but knew she would prevail. Looking on, Julie smiled, realizing how well Dennis understood her sister.

Although he had volunteered for kitchen duty, Julie thought that Dennis was unusually quiet. He stood at the sink, scraping plates and scrubbing pots, working steadily and thoroughly. But he did not enter into the family banter in the way he usually did. Ted was in the kitchen, too, which meant that there was a constant stream of humor. Dennis seemed not to notice most of it. She knew him well enough to recognize that his mind was on something else. What was he so distracted about? she wondered.

At last the job was done. The only dishes still out were a stack of clean pie plates and coffee cups.

Dennis looped a drenched dish towel through the handle of the refrigerator and glanced up at Julie. "How about a walk, Julie?"

Involuntarily her eyes darted to the window. "It's dark and probably cold."

He took her hand. "That's okay. If we keep moving, we'll keep warm."

She sensed some nervousness in him. Perhaps if she went for a walk she would find out what was going on.

In their warmest coats, they stepped outside the front door and began walking down the sidewalk. As was their habit, they held hands. Dennis was still strangely quiet. They had gone more than a block before he said anything.

"I like being with your family," he told her. "They're very comfortable to be around."

Julie was skeptical. "Even Marjorie?"

Dennis smiled and said, "Well. . .for the most part. I wasn't too keen on that apron."

"I could tell. But you were a good sport."

"It's nice that your grandmother was here."

"Yes." Julie sensed that Dennis was working his way up to something with all this small talk. "I was going to go get her, but Ted wanted to do it."

"It has been a nice day."

"Yes, it has been."

They were quiet again for another block.

"Julie, I have to break a promise."

She looked at him, questioning. "You mean you're not going to proofread my term paper?"

Dennis was serious. "No, it's more than that." His pace slowed. "I want you to marry me."

"I know you do, Dennis. You've been saying that for a year."

"I don't want to wait six months to decide whether we're going to do it."

"Oh."

"When I agreed to a moratorium on talking about marriage, things were different. I didn't have this opportunity in Seattle hanging over my head. And I guess I hadn't realized what it would feel like to be this close to graduating and moving on into the next phase of my life."

"So. . .what are you saying?"

With his free hand, he reached into his jacket pocket and withdrew a small box. "I'm saying I want you to have this."

Julie gasped. Dennis had surprised her. Obviously the box held a ring. She never thought he would go that far until she had agreed to marry him.

They stopped walking and stood under a street light as he opened the box and showed her the contents. The diamond was small, but exquisitely set. It was similar to one that she had once remarked on when they passed a jewelry store at the mall. That had been a long time ago. She was surprised he remembered.

He took the ring from its cushion and held it between them. Even under the street light, it sparkled. Instinctively, Julie reached out to touch it. It was truly beautiful.

"Julie Covington, will you marry me?"

She looked into his green eyes. He was so devoted, so sure, so perfect for her.

"Dennis, I don't know what to say."

"It's supposed to be an easy question. Say yes."

"When we agreed not to discuss marriage for a while. . . well, I just haven't been thinking in those terms lately. My mind has been on so many other things."

"That's fair enough." Dennis gently set the ring back in the box and snapped it shut. "I'm the one who broke our agreement. So I guess first I should ask you to lift the moratorium."

Julie swallowed nervously. They had already come three months through the six months that she had asked for. Before too much longer she would have to give Dennis an answer anyway.

"Okay," she said. "The subject is once again open for discussion."

"Good. I'd really like to announce our engagement at Christmas."

"Christmas?"

"Yes. Then we could get married right after you finish school in May." His eyes searched hers for some sign of encouragement.

"I still need some time."

"I see." Dennis turned away and resumed walking, a few

steps ahead of Julie.

"Dennis, please try to understand," Julie pleaded. She hurried her steps to be beside him again.

"I am. I have for a long time."

"Yes, and I'm grateful for it. Please, just a little more time."

"You keep saying you need more time but you never say how much," Dennis said with no softness in his voice. "Even if I had waited the full six months before bringing the subject up again, I have no guarantee that you wouldn't ask for more time."

Julie had no respone. What he said was true.

"Maybe your sister is right," Dennis said angrily. "Maybe you artist types just don't have your feet on the ground."

Julie stopped abruptly and yanked on his arm to make him look at her. "You take that back!" She sounded like one of her malcontent nieces, but she meant what she said.

Dennis looked away and muttered, "I'm sorry."

"I don't want to fight, Dennis."

"Neither do I."

"Please, be patient just a little longer."

Dennis looked at Julie and put his arm around her shoulders. "Julie, I love you. And those blue eyes get to me every time. I can't turn you down. I'll keep waiting."

Julie sighed with relief. "So you're not angry?" She thought he had every right to be.

He shook his head. "Disappointed, but not angry."

"I'm sorry."

"Hey, it is getting cold out here. Let's head back."

Julie took the cue and changed the subject. "Dad probably has a fire going by now."

They walked home quickly and ducked through the front door just as Ted and Tom were whooping over a touchdown on TV. Grammy sat in her armchair with a distant smile on her face. Julie stopped to kiss the top of her head before going to the closet with their coats.

Marjorie set aside her magazine. "We were just talking about pie and coffee. Are you two ready?"

"Yep," said Dennis, with his usual cheerful tone. "Anytime."

"Good." Marjorie got up off the couch. "We have pumpkin, mincemeat, and dutch apple."

"I'll have one of each." He started following her toward the kitchen.

"Don't be ridiculous. You'll make yourself sick."

"I thought it was an American tradition to make yourself sick on Thanksgiving."

Julie sat on the arm of the couch as she watched Marjorie and Dennis traipse toward the kitchen to serve pie. She had a lump in her throat. What was holding her back from Dennis?

thirteen

November gave way to December. The days grew short and dark. The shimmering light that Julie loved to capture on canvas was difficult to find. On the weekends she worked in her garage studio, painting from memory of the summer sun.

Lovellton and all of Chicagoland braced itself for the onslaught of winter. An immobilizing snowfall could come at any time, paralyzing the region and inflicting irreparable damage on the biggest retail season of the year. Perhaps that was why so many people were in such a hurry for Christmas. Rooftops all over town began sporting reindeer and lights. Trees appeared in the department stores, covered with tinsel and the latest designer ornaments. Peppy, tinny Christmas music was piped through sound systems everywhere. Going to the mall required an extra dose of fortitude.

Julie loved Christmas. The music, the lights, the special church services—even the crowds. It was the one time of the year that she did not mind having snow on the ground. Icicles hanging from the trees and a layer of white across the lawn seemed somehow acceptable at Christmastime. The sun was not brilliant like it was in the summer, but the snow and ice magnified what the sun offered, transforming Lovellton into a winter wonderland.

But this year, Julie was less enthusiastic. Thanksgiving normally marked the beginning of a festive season, but this year it heralded pensive reflection for Julie. Dennis would not wait much longer, she feared. And she should not ask him to. She had to come to a decision.

Julie rinsed out the brush she had been using, watching the bright blue fade away into the cleaning fluid. As she wiped her hands on a damp rag, she stood back to look at her day's work. It was an impulsive start on a portrait of Della Paxton. She had skipped over the preliminary sketches she usually did and went straight to work on a fresh canvas. Already Della's silver hair was sparkling against a subtle blue background.

Julie did not know what made her start work on such a project. It was completely unplanned. But something had put her in the mood to do it, so she had. If the end result proved good enough, she might send it to Larry for Christmas. He genuinely admired her painting; he would appreciate the gesture as few others could.

Julie hung her rag on a hook. As she did, her eyes fell on the stack of canvases that Larry had perused during his brief visit. She remembered the look of wonder in his eyes—not surprise that she could paint so well, but the wonder of admiration and appreciation. She never saw that look on Dennis's face. He looked at her paintings occasionally and commented politely, but it was not the same as the reaction Larry had had.

A glance at her watch reminded Julie that the project would have to wait for further progress. It was late, and she needed to get back to school. She snapped the light off, locked the door, and returned to the house to gather her things.

Grammy had already gone to bed, but Julie wanted to check on her one last time. Stealthily, she opened the bedroom door. The light from the hall illuminated her grandmother's sleeping face. She looked peaceful and innocent.

"Grammy," Julie whispered. "You always knew what you wanted. I wish you could help me sort things out now."

Her grandmother's only reply was her soft, steady breathing.

Snowflakes crystallized instantly on the window and shimmered in the sunlight. Swirled around by the gentle wind, they formed wispy, glistening patterns against the glass.

Julienne stood in the waiting lounge on the pediatrics floor, watching the snow. Christmas would be here soon enough and everyone would be wishing for a sparkling white blanket. Children would romp through the snow, roll it in their hands, and throw it at each other—and anyone else who dared pass by. Their parents would keep the fires stoked and something hot to drink on the back burner of the stove.

Despite the snow and the cold that brought it, the afternoon was a fine one. The fall term was nearly done; Julienne had received good reports from her instructors and was once again near the top of her class. Colin was proud of her, but more important, she was proud of herself. She still had hesitancies about whether she would ever have the right instincts for nursing, but her academic accomplishments were beginning to outweigh her fears.

The high point of the day had been seeing Thomas. After being in the hospital for several weeks, he had finally gone home. He was far from mended, but he was well enough to go home where his mother could look after him. Colin's only condition was that she bring him in for weekly checkups. Julienne had been in the room when Colin told Mary MacEnzie that she could take her little boy home and she was nearly as excited as Mary. She had worn herself out sitting in his room, studying under a dim light and scurrying back into the dormitory before curfew. At first the fear of another crisis was constant. When Thomas had stabilized, Julienne marveled at the improvement she saw every day and plunged into her textbooks with renewed vigor for learning how to be a nurse. Being with Thomas was ebbing away the doubt that had plagued her. This small child, whom she would never have met had he not fallen before her eyes, was having a profound effect on her future. Never again did she want to be caught unprepared to handle a crisis.

Thomas had been in to see Colin earlier in the afternoon for his weekly checkup, looking rosy and vibrant and bursting to be rid of the cast still on his leg. Seeing him in the hall, looking so well, had cheered Julienne more than anything else in weeks.

She felt a presence behind her and turned to see Colin. She smiled at him contentedly.

"Nice afternoon," he said, following her gaze out the window.

"Picture perfect."

"Too bad we have to be in here."

Julienne glanced at a clock. "Not much longer for me. How about you?"

"I'm afraid I'll be here all night."

"But you came in very early today."

"I'm covering for someone."

She looked at him gently. "The other interns always know who to ask when they need time off."

He smiled shyly. "Perhaps I am an easy target. I just can't help it." His expression sobered. "Julienne, there is something I've been meaning to discuss with you."

"Yes?"

"About the holidays."

Julienne nodded. "My mother is expecting me home."

"I thought so. My parents are hoping I will come home, too, since I didn't make it home in the summer. But I don't think I can go."

"Oh?"

"The schedule around here is just too heavy to get away for that long. I could manage two or three days, perhaps, but that's not really enough to go all the way to Maine and back."

She looked at him sternly and furrowed her brow. "Are you

sure you didn't agree to fill in for someone else over Christmas?"

Grinning, he shook his head. "I promise I did no such thing. None of the interns will have more than a couple of days off."

"Well, then I guess you won't be going home to Seabridge."

"Afraid not. But I'll be glad to see you off when you go. I'm sure I can get someone to cover for a couple of hours."

Julienne pursed her lips and turned away from the window. "I'm not sure I want to go."

He looked at her surprised. "But it's Christmas. Don't you want to be with your family?"

"Yes, and no. I miss them, of course. My brothers are growing up so fast. Seeing Thomas always make me miss them. But. . ."

"But. . .what?"

"My life is here now. In some ways this feels more like home than Seabridge does."

"It's just school, Julienne, not family."

She had hoped he would understand more readily. "I'm just not sure," she said noncommitally as she sank into a chair.

Colin sat beside her. "We've become good friends, haven't we?"

She nodded eagerly.

"Let me ask you a question as a friend."

"Sure." She looked at him expectantly.

"Are you avoiding your mother?"

"Why would I—"

He waved away her objections. "She never wanted you to be here, to study nursing. And you almost didn't come back in September. I can understand that you might be afraid what would happen if you go home now."

Julienne looked at the floor as he continued speaking.

"It's not my place to tell you what to do, any more than it is your mother's place. You're a grown woman, and you can make your own decisions. But you do need to face your mother sooner or later."

"I choose later," she muttered.

"Don't make light of this, Julienne," he reprimanded.

He had never used such a tone with her before, and it took her by surprise. Not knowing what to say, she just looked at him, puzzled.

"I'm sorry," he said softly. "I should not have spoken so harshy. . .perhaps not at all."

"No, don't be sorry. You are my friend. I like to know your thoughts. If you think I should go home for Christmas, maybe I should think about it some more."

"I don't want to say I think you should go home or not go home. That's your decision. I just don't think you should make that decision out of fear."

She nodded and looked down at her nervous hands. "I understand. I promise to think about it."

"Have you made a reservation yet?"

"Mother has. Her last letter said that she would send me the ticket."

"That's probably wise. The trains will be very full at Christmas." He looked at his watch. "I've got to get back."

"Me, too. I have one more class today."

He stood up and offered his hand. Julienne took it and let him pull her to her feet. At the softness of his hand, a strange wave of emotion surged through her. He held her hand for a moment longer than necessary, then dropped it awkwardly.

"I'll see you later, then," she said, moving toward the hallway.

"Yes. I'll phone you in a couple of days when I have some free time."

She nodded and gave a little wave as he turned to the left and she went to the right.

She had not expected such a reaction from him at the mention of not going to Maine for Christmas. She was only half-serious about it when she said she might not go. She had assumed all along that she would go, especially since her mother was forging ahead with plans. If she did not go, it would be the first Christmas of her life away from her family.

While she got more of a break than the interns did, it was an awfully long way to go for just a few days. At the most she would have only five days at home.

Colin was right. Eventually she was going to have to work things out with her mother. In her heart, she did not think she could ever forgive her mother for chasing Lorenzo away. Things would never be the same between them, but surely they could come to a more peaceable understanding than they had now.

But Colin was right about something else, too. She should not make the decision out of fear, fear of the consequences of going home or fear of the consequences of not going home. She would have to find another basis for her decision, and she would have to find it soon.

&

Two days later, Julienne's train ticket arrived in the mail. It was the only piece of mail she received that day. Mrs. Davis had laid it on a table at the foot of the stairs where all the students picked up mail, and Julienne saw it as soon as she came through the doorway. She knew from the size of the envelope what it contained. Her mother's familiar, bold, heavy handwriting transmitted a clear message that she wanted her daughter home for Christmas. The envelope held no letter, just the train ticket.

"Not bad news, I hope." Amy, a fellow student was sprawled on the couch in the lobby, looking at a magazine. She looked up at Julienne.

Julienne forced a smile. "No, no bad news." She waved the envelope. "My train ticket home for Christmas."

"That's great. You're lucky to have it." She sounded envious.

"Weren't you able to get a reservation?"

Amy shook her head. "There wasn't much left after paying the tuition. New Jersey is just too far to go."

"Oh. I'm sorry," Julienne said.

Her friend shrugged. "I stayed here last year, too. It's not so bad."

"But your family. . . How long has it been since you saw them?"

"Almost two years. Is your boyfriend going home, too?"

Julienne was taken off guard. "Boyfriend?"

"You know, Dr. Covington."

"He's just a friend. We're from the same hometown, that's all."

Amy looked skeptical, but nodded. Julienne did not want to pursue the discussion further.

"Guess I'd better go study," she said weakly.

Dragging her feet, Julienne pulled herself up the stairs to the quiet of her own room. Not bothering even to take off her coat, she sat on the bed and stared at the ticket in her hand. Should she go to Maine? There were more reasons to go than not to go, she supposed, but still she felt uneasy about it. If she made the obvious decision, she might be unhappy about it; if she made another choice, she would have to be ready to face the consequences.

If only Colin had been able to go home. It would have been so much easier knowing that he was in Seabridge, too. Despite what she had said to Amy just a few minutes ago, Colin was not just a friend. He was her truest friend, the one who believed in her when she did not believe in herself, the one who helped her see beyond the present moment to what she might someday be.

The plain fact was that she did not want to leave Colin

behind. She could never say that to him directly, but she knew it was true. The thought of him, spending Christmas in Chicago, alone, probably working too many hours at the hospital. . . She pushed the picture out of her mind.

Julienne was restless, too restless to study. She stood up, pulled off her coat, kicked off her shoes, and removed her belt. Perhaps if she got comfortable she could settle down. She snapped on the light at her desk and opened a book.

It was no use. All she saw was the image of the train ticket, alternating with a picture of Colin, looking haggard and overworked.

Suddenly, she knew what she wanted to do. She snatched the ticket off the bed and briskly walked out into the hall and down the stairs. Amy was still sitting on the couch in the lobby, this time with a textbook in her lap.

"Amy, I want you to go home for Christmas."

"What are you talking about?"

Julienne thrust the train ticket toward her. "If you try right away, perhaps you can still get a reservation. You can exchange my ticket for one to New Jersey."

Amy stared at the ticket, hanging limp in the air between them. "I can't take your ticket."

"I want you to." Julienne waved it closer to Amy.

"What will you do?"

"Stay here."

"But why? What about your family."

"I'll miss them, but I have my reasons. Please accept this ticket."

Stunned, Amy reached up and took the ticket from Julienne's hand.

There was no turning back now.

fourteen

"Auggh! I'm never going to be ready for this test!" said Melanie, Julie's roommate, as she dropped her book bag on the floor and flopped backwards onto her bed. Julie looked up from her own studies at her dramatic friend.

"What's the matter?" Julie asked. Taking advantage of the interruption, she reached into her desk drawer for a teabag and plugged in her hot pot to heat water.

"There's just too much material. Dr. Foxx is asking for blood in that theology class."

"I thought you liked that class."

"I do. The discussions are interesting. But this exam counts for fifty percent of my grade."

"You need a break. Drive into town. Get away from campus for a while."

"Are you nuts?" Melanie pulled herself off the bed. "No time for fun. The test is at eight o'clock tomorrow morning. I'll be up half the night as it is." She retrieved her book bag, plopped it on the desk, and started unloading it.

"At least have some tea with me." Julie could see Melanie softening. "I have apple cinnamon, your favorite," she prodded.

"All right, one cup of tea, then I'm back at it." Melanie seemed to relax a little bit. "How are you doing? When's your first final?"

"Tomorrow afternoon. Then two the next day." Julie shrugged. "I'm studying, of course, but I'm not panicking. Not yet, anyway."

Melanie shrugged off her jacket, letting it fall to the floor with no intention of hanging it properly. "Well, I am," she said. "I've been working on theology so much I haven't started on anything else."

"Either you know it or you don't, Mel. I don't believe in all-night cramming. It's better to get some rest."

Melanie sank into her desk chair. "It's a choice between two evils. Staying up all night or flunking the exam."

"Stop being so dramatic. You're not going to flunk." Julie poured the hot water over the teabags in their mugs. "If you didn't already know that stuff, you would never have been able to keep up with the class discussions like you have."

Melanie gratefully accepted a steaming mug from Julie. "I admit it; I'm a wreck. I just don't know any other way to get through finals."

"This is your last year. It's almost over and you won't ever have to do it again."

"I can't believe we're seniors. And I can't believe Dennis is finishing now. I'm so jealous. Has he made up his mind which job to take, yet?"

Julie stiffened slightly. "If he has, he hasn't told me."

"What's the matter with you two?" Melanie spooned too much honey into her tea.

"What do you mean?" Julie asked guardedly.

"Don't the two of you ever talk to each other?"

"Of course we do. This is a small campus. We see each other every day."

"But do you talk? He's had his choice of jobs for weeks. He must have a preference."

"Well, I guess he prefers the one in Seattle."

"But. . .?"

"But nothing." Julie nervously started straightening the papers on her desk. "He just hasn't made a final decision yet."

"Why not?"

"I don't know." She was starting to squirm in her chair.

"Are you two going to get engaged soon?"

"I don't know." Before Julie's eyes floated the image of the ring Dennis had wanted to put on her finger at Thanksgiving.

Melanie said, "Well, if you don't know, who does?"

"Let's not analyze my relationship with Dennis right now, okay? Let's just have our tea and get back to studying."

"But this is so much more interesting."

"Not for me."

"You told me I should relax for a while. I'm relaxing."

"Melanie!"

"Okay, okay. I get the message."

They turned back to their books. The words swam in front of Julie's eyes. She had lost her concentration. In her usual forthright way, Melanie had asked the questions that troubled Julie the most. And she was no closer to finding the answers than when Dennis had proposed on Thanksgiving evening.

Thinking that she might be able to concentrate if she made a fresh start on studying for a different exam, Julie closed the sociology textbook in front of her and opened an art history one. She riffled the pages to find the place where she had left off. As she did so, a little card slid from among the pages. She recognized it right away—it was the card Larry had sent her after he went back to Maine in October.

> *Dear Julie,*
>
> *Thank you for a delightful day in Lovellton. It was good to see you in your real setting and have a better understanding of what your life is like. Meeting your grandmother was a pleasure. You have a wonderful family, but I can see the stress that you have all been under.*

*I especially enjoyed seeing your paintings. I've al-
ready got the two I bought from you framed and hanging on the second floor landing. God has given you
such a penetrating gift.*

*That makes three Julie Covington originals that we
have hanging at Leed House. I hope there will be many
more to come.*

*In fact, I hope to see more of you, too. When will
you be coming back to Maine?*

Warm regards,

Larry

On one level it was a simple note acknowledging their day
together. It was polite and encouraging. But Julie knew Larry
well enough to know that he did not waste words to be polite
and encouraging. The note was not really necessary at all,
but he had sent it.

And he had not mentioned his mother anywhere in the letter. Always before Larry had used Della as a reason to contact Julie and had said how much his mother would be glad to
hear news of her. But the letter was silent about Della. Larry
was talking simply of himself. What did this all mean?

Julie swiftly slid the note card into a desk drawer and closed
it. You're making too much of it, she told herself. Get a grip
on things.

The phone in the hall rang. Melanie popped up to answer it
and promptly stuck her head back in and said, "It's for you.
Long distance."

Julie rarely spoke to anyone long distance. It had to be a
call from Maine.

"Hello?"

"Hi, Julie. It's Larry."

Unconsciously, Julie blushed. It was as if he knew that she

had just been thinking about him.

"How are you, Larry? Has the weather turned cold?"

"Subzero, I'm afraid. We already have snow on the ground. But I didn't call to talk about the weather." Excitement filled his voice.

"What's going on?" Julie could not imagine what he would be calling her about. But she was glad to hear his voice.

"I took your paintings to someone the other day."

"What do you mean?"

"To a friend who runs an art gallery."

"An art gallery?" She was incredulous. "I'm not ready for that kind of thing."

"He thinks you are, Julie. He wants to see more of your work."

"What for?"

Larry laughed. "To sell, of course."

"Sell?" Julie could not believe what she was hearing.

"Right. He's got the biggest art gallery in the county. It's in a very chic area where there is a lot of tourist business all year round. It's a great oppportunity for you."

"I don't know what to say."

"Julie, you're a gifted artist. Why don't you believe in yourself?"

It was a good question; she wished she knew the answer. "I don't know. It never seemed practical to be an artist. Everyone else has always treated my art like a hobby."

"It's no hobby, Julie. I don't care what your sister says, I think you have a marketable skill in what you do with a paint brush. And this is proof."

Julie had to laugh aloud. "Marjorie will never believe this." The shock was wearing off a bit. "So what do I need to do? Just choose a painting to send to Maine?"

"I tried to remember as many as I could and told him about

them. He suggested that you send photographs and he could select about half a dozen."

"Half a dozen?"

"Based on what he's seen so far, he's very optimistic. Oh, and you might send photocopies of some of your sketches, too. Some of them would look pretty nice if they were properly framed."

"This is incredible."

"Will you do it?"

"I'd be a fool not to!"

"Great! I'll send some information on my friend through the mail and you can work out the details with him."

"Okay. Thank you!"

"My pleasure. Hey, how are your exams going?"

From there, the conversation turned to more mundane matters. Julie kept expecting that Larry would hang up. She had never known him to be so chatty, but she enjoyed talking to him. She had been nervous before his visit, but that feeling was gone. A genuine friendship had emerged somewhere along the line.

When she finally hung up, she looked at her watch and realized that she had been talking for an hour—and that she was going to be late meeting Dennis for dinner at the dining commons. She scurried back to her room and grabbed her parka off the bed.

"What's going on?" Melanie asked.

"Tell ya later. I'm supposed to meet Dennis."

Julie could tell Melanie had a dozen more questions. Probably she had overheard much of Julie's end of the phone conversation. But right now was not the time for explanations. Besides, she had no idea what she would say.

❧

"I'd just about given up on you," Dennis said as she pushed

open the door to the dining commons and found him standing nearby.

"Sorry. Had a phone call from Maine. Somebody wants to buy some of my paintings!"

Dennis raised his eyebrows and his eyes widened. "Really? Someone wants your pictures?"

They moved toward the line, picking up trays and silverware. Julie ignored the mild irritation she felt at his surprise that someone would show interest in her art.

"Larry knows the guy and he says it is a genuine offer."

"Larry? The guy from last summer?"

Julie inspected the entree choices and gestured toward the meatloaf. "I guess I never told you that he took a couple of my paintings back with him after he was here in October."

"No, you never mentioned that."

"Sorry." Julie was not sure why she had never bothered to tell Dennis about Larry's interest in her art. Perhaps it was because she did not want to raise her own hopes by sharing that information. Or perhaps she just wanted to have a bond with Larry that did not involve Dennis. She decided that this was not the time to analyze her past actions and picked up a bowl of red Jello.

They found a booth and sat down across from each other.

"I had a phone call from Seattle today," Dennis said quietly.

"Oh?"

"They want an answer."

Julie pressed her lips together and avoided eye contact. No doubt Dennis wanted an answer, too. "What are you going to tell them?" she asked.

He spoke slowly. "I'm inclined to accept. It's unlikely I would get another offer this attractive."

"Then you should take it."

"I probably will, unless. . ."

Julie put a piece of meat in her mouth and chewed it slowly. She knew what he would say next.

"Unless you give me a good reason not to." Dennis completed his sentence. "I'd like to think you would be happy living in Seattle, although it is a long way from your family. You'd be free to paint and sketch as much as you like without having to worry about marketability."

Julie set her fork down and put her hands in her lap. Suddenly she had no appetite. She could feel the color draining from her face.

"Maybe I would like to think about marketability," she said.

"Then fine, try to sell your paintings. Whatever you want."

"It doesn't matter to you one way or another, does it?"

"What do you mean?"

"Whether I sell any paintings or not. Doesn't that matter to you?"

Dennis was bewildered. "Whatever will make you happy."

"Don't you think my art is good enough to sell?"

"I'm no art critic, Julie."

"I'm not asking you to be an art expert. I just want you to believe in my work."

"I do!" Dennis defended himself.

"No," Julie said with sudden insight. "You believe in letting me do whatever will make me happy."

"Is there something wrong with that?"

"It's not the same as believing in my work."

"I'm lost, Julie. What are you talking about?"

"Never mind," Julie muttered. Dennis did everything according to a plan. What she was feeling at the moment was too abstract to fit into his plan. She shoved her Jello around in the bowl.

They were silent for a long time, neither of them eating

much. But the unanswered questions hung thickly in the air between them.

"I still have the ring," Dennis finally said. "We could still announce our engagement at Christmas."

"Dennis, please. . . ," Julie nearly groaned.

"We can't keep doing this, Julie. Either you love me enough to marry me or you don't."

"It's such a big decision. I want to feel really sure. Why don't you go to Seattle, and we can write and phone each other. I have to stay here till I graduate in the spring, anyway. We don't have to rush this."

Dennis's voice was low and controlled. "Julie, we've been seeing each other exclusively for two and a half years. We said we loved each other almost from the start. I asked you to marry me a year ago, and you wanted more time. I would hardly say that we are rushing into anything."

Julie sighed and forced herself to look at him directly. "I'm sorry, Dennis. I care for you so much, but I just can't say yes yet. My life is too muddled right now. I'm not sure I'm making good choices about anything these days. I've never been good at making decisions under pressure."

For a long time neither of them said anything. Julie picked at her Jello but did not really eat anything. Finally, Dennis spoke.

"I've been thinking about this a lot, Julie. I can honestly say that I've made every effort to be patient because I know you've been stressed out for the last few months."

"I appreciate your understanding."

"But. . .something has to change. I can't go on wearing my feelings about you on my sleeve and never being sure that you feel the same way."

"You know I love you."

"Do you? I'm not so sure. I used to think it was enough that

I was madly in love with you, but I see now that it isn't."

"What are you saying, Dennis?"

"I think we should break up."

"Break up?" It sounded so final.

"Yes. I'm going to take that job in Seattle. But I won't be writing or phoning."

"But, Dennis—"

"I really think this is the best way, Julie. I love you, but I just don't have it in me to do this anymore. I've prayed and prayed. First I prayed that you would decide to marry me. When that didn't happen, I prayed that God would show me whether or not we really belong together. I think I have my answer."

Tears were filling Julie's eyes, but she refused to cry in the middle of the dining commons. Dennis could at least have picked a more private place for this confrontation.

"I'll miss you. I'll miss your family. I'll even miss Marjorie, the mother hen. But I think this is the right thing. You have to be completely free to work out whatever it is that's tying you in knots. I'm just in the way. And I'm not very good at living in an emotional limbo."

Julie's eyes fell back to the table. "I'm so sorry, Dennis. I never meant for you to be hit with the fallout of my problems."

"I know."

They were silent again. Then Dennis started gathering up their dishes on his tray. He looked at her mournfully and said simply, "I love you, Julie. Goodbye."

And he took their trays and put them through the window into the dishwashing room, just like he had done hundreds of other times.

Life has to go on.

fifteen

Julie lost interest in studying for her finals and had to, quite literally, depend on her own theory that either she knew the material or she did not.

It had never occurred to her that Dennis would simply give up on her. He had always said he would wait for her for as long as it took. Julie assumed that the future of their relationship was in her own hands. . .that she might be the one to eventually walk away.

She knew she had given him every reason to do what he did. If she looked at the situation through his eyes, she had to admit that it had not been easy. They had a comfortable enough relationship for what it was. They shared some classes, studied together much of the time, shared a common taste in music, passed popular novels back and forth between them. They were together habitually and predictably all over the campus. Going from a student habit, though a genuinely fond one, to an enduring relationship had been more and more difficult to do as graduation grew closer.

Julie had balked and never seemed to be able to step toward her own future. Dennis was only one piece of the puzzle that dominated her life, only one of a series of question marks that seemed to have no answers. Why had her grandmother been struck with a debilitating illness? Why did God give her a gift for art but not more confidence in developing it? Why did she struggle against the inevitable changes she faced at this juncture of her life? Often it seemed like she was making no progress at all toward resolving these questions. It was no wonder that Dennis had finally had enough.

As soon as her finals were over, half-hearted as her effort was, Julie packed a small bag and headed home for a couple of weeks.

At first she did not say anything to her family about Dennis. She let references to him fly past with no response and did not bring up his name herself. Because of his absence, Marjorie jumped to the conclusion that Dennis had gone home to be with his own family in Colorado. That was, in fact, the truth. What Marjorie did not know was the reason for his choice, and Julie kept her silence on that point.

Christmas Eve came and the family gathered. It was their long-standing tradition to trim the tree together on Christmas Eve. Giving in to pressure from her children years ago, Liz Covington had begun allowing a smaller tree in the family room earlier in December. But this was the official Covington tree, standing nearly nine feet tall, bearing the heirloom ornaments, and dominating the spacious living room. The fragrance of the towering pine permeated the house from the moment Ted and Tom gleefully carried in their prize. Their father-son jaunt to cut a fresh tree was a tradition they both cherished. Ted used to say that it was the one time each year when the boys could get away from all the girls in the house. Every year, while the men were gone for several hours looking for the perfect tree, the women sorted through ornaments and trimmings, putting last minute touches on festive decorations around the house.

After the tree was securely in its stand and he was sure it was steady, Ted had gone to Prairie Valley Nursing Center to get his grandmother. Now Grammy sat in the armchair in the living room where she always sat at Christmastime, with a clear view of the tree. She used to help the children fill in the bare spots with shiny glass balls. Julie missed Grammy's active participation but was glad even for her silent presence.

"I bought a new ornament, Grammy," Julie said as she pressed a soft, round, handstitched ornament into her grandmother's hand.

Grammy rubbed the stitches around the edge between her forefinger and thumb and smiled. "Sov. . . ."

"Yes, it's soft," Julie said. "And very pretty, don't you think?"

Grammy stared up at the tree and grinned.

Marjorie's daughters scampered into the room. "Can we help? Can we help?"

"Of course you can," Liz said, handing them each an ornament. "These were your mother's ornaments when she was a little girl."

"We know that, Grandma," one of them said. "You tell us every year."

"Repeating myself is part of the Christmas tradition. Now get busy." She shooed them toward the tree with the heirloom ornaments.

"We need music," Tom said and snapped a compact disk into its slot on the stereo. A brass quintet added its celebration to the household.

"This is more like it," Marjorie said, stretching to place ornaments where her children could not reach. "Too bad about Dennis."

Julie's head snapped up from the tray of favorite ornaments. What did her sister know? "What do you mean?" she asked casually.

"We've gotten used to having him around on the holidays, that's all. It's nice that he could go be with his family, but we miss him."

Julie nodded, silently.

"Why didn't you go with him?"

Julie tried to busy herself looking for a particular ornament. "Well, I. . ."

"You probably wanted to be here," Marjorie said. "But
you and Dennis might not always live around here. What if
you move to Seattle? And with his family in Colorado, you
can expect to visit your in-laws for the holidays sometimes."

"I don't think that's going to be a problem," Julie muttered
as she hung a silver star.

"You'd be surprised at what's involved in juggling two fami-
lies."

Ted playfully edged Julie out of her spot in front of the tree.
"So are you going to call him tomorrow, or what?"

"I don't think so."

"Of course you will," Marjorie insisted. "How can you not
talk to each other on Christmas?"

Julie turned around and faced her family squarely. "Because we're not really talking to each other at all."

Marjorie gasped.

"Have you and Dennis been quarreling?" Liz asked.

"Not exactly," Julie said. "We just decided not to see each
other anymore."

Everyone froze and stared at her.

"That's absurd," Marjorie blurted. "What are you talking
about?"

"Just what I said. Dennis and I have broken up."

"Oh, honey," Liz said, rising to take her daugher in her
arms. "After all this time. The two of you were so close."

Julie accepted her mother's comfort for only a moment and
then said, "I'm okay. I think it is the best thing, actually. We
probably should have broken up months ago."

"Oh, that's ridiculous," Marjorie said. "You two are perfect for each other. Whatever happened, you should work it
out."

"No, Marjorie," Julie said firmly. "This is it. There's nothing to work out."

"I don't believe that. The two of you could have a very nice future together. Why don't you call him?"

"Marjorie, please," Julie said desperately.

"Can it, Marjorie." Ted's voice rang out authoritatively. "Julie is not you. She can run her own life."

Julie shot her brother a grateful glance and changed the subject. "I just saw the mailman go by. Looked like he had quite a stack of cards for us."

The girls abandoned their posts at the tree and raced to the front door to check the mailbox. "I want to get the mail!" one wailed.

"I'm going to do it!"

"No! I got here first."

"Mom! She won't let me get the mail!"

They finally returned with fairly evenly divided stacks and started reading out names. "Grandpa, Grandpa, Grandpa and Grandma, Uncle Ted—hey, you don't live here. Why did the mailman leave your mail here?"

"Because he knew I would be here today."

"He did not!"

"Just give me my card, please."

The little girl complied. "Here's some for you, Aunt Julie. Three of them."

"Thanks." Julie glanced at the handwriting and saw that two of the cards were from college friends who had graduated last year and moved away. The third was in a less familiar script, but she had the nagging feeling she should recognize it. She flipped it over and looked at the return address on the back. "L. Paxton," it said, giving Larry's address in Seabridge, Maine.

Julie glanced around the room nervously. Everyone was

absorbed in the cards and ornaments.

"Look, Tom," her mother said, "we finally heard from the Nelsons. I never had their new address after they moved."

"Here's one from Dr. Krueger," Tom said. "I heard he had a heart attack last summer."

No one noticed that Julie slipped from the room and went up the stairs to her own room. She had finished the portrait of Della and sent it to Larry, but he could not have received it yet. So this was not a thank you note. She was more than curious. Julie laid the cards from her school friends aside and carefully opened the one from Maine. She had already received a card signed by Della and Larry and had sent one addressed to both of them. This envelope from Larry was a surprise.

The illustration on the front of the card was a winter night scene. Fresh, pure white snow swirled in the bluish light streaming from a lone star in the sky. Inside, the card simply said, "May the light of Christ be yours this Christmas."

Larry had added a personal note.

> *Dear Julie,*
> *I saw this card and thought of you. It reminds me of the light in your paintings, light aching to be set free and shine boldly.*
> *Warmly,*
> *Larry.*

Warmly, Larry. Julie silently repeated the words to herself. It was unnecessary for Larry to send her a card, much less to write a personal note. Warmly, Larry. What did that mean? Light aching to be set free. In those six words, Larry communicated that he understood what her paintings were all about. Was it a coincidence of words, or an intentional expression?

Knock, knock. She heard knuckles rapping on her door and knew that Ted wanted to talk. He was the one member of the family most likely to follow her upstairs, so she was not surprised that he had appeared. She stuffed the envelope and card under her pillow.

"Come in," she called.

Ted stuck his head in the door. "You okay?"

"Sure. Why not?"

"Don't give me that line, Julie." Ted closed the door behind him and sat down on the bed next to his little sister. "You and Dennis were pretty thick. Even if breaking up was the right thing to do, you must be feeling something."

Julie pulled her knees up to her chest and propped her chin on them. She could trust Ted. "Well, at first I was shocked. He's the one who decided to call it quits, and I never thought he would do that."

"Wasn't he hounding you to get married?"

She nodded. "I wasn't ready to say yes. I thought the option would always be there. But he got tired of waiting."

"Are you sorry now that you didn't say yes?"

"No. Not really. I probably should have just said no a long time ago and not put him through so much."

"The last thing I want to do is sound like Marjorie," Ted said, "but I'm as blown away as she is. I didn't know there was anything wrong between you and Dennis."

Julie unfolded her legs and stood up. "That's the problem," she said, pacing slowly toward the window. "There wasn't anything really wrong. We enjoyed each other's company and hardly ever argued, except about whether or not to get married. And I know he loves me."

"But?"

"But he wants to take care of me. He thinks it is enough if he has a good job so I can be free to paint as much as I want to."

"What's so bad about that? Isn't that what every artist wants?"

Julie rubbed her forehead. "On the surface, yes. But I don't want to be indulged. Ever since last summer I've been trying to figure out if I have a future as an artist."

"Everyone knows you're talented."

"Lots of people are talented. Not everyone succeeds."

"And if you married Dennis?"

"Then it wouldn't matter if I succeed. He thinks it would be enough that I am free to paint."

"Wouldn't that be art for art's sake? Or have you fallen into Marjorie's trap of always thinking about marketability?"

Julie perched on the window seat and picked up her childhood teddy bear. "It's not a question of marketability. It's a question of how much I believe in myself. . .and how much Dennis believes in me. I couldn't say yes to him and spend the rest of my life wondering if he believes in me of if he's just indulging me so that he'll have a happy wife."

"These are subtle points, Julie."

"I know. But if Dennis is not saying yes to all of me, then how can I say yes to him?"

"I guess you can't."

"Dennis finally figured that out, I suppose. He realized before I did that I was never going to say yes, so he withdrew his standing offer."

"So how do you feel now?"

"At first I was shocked, of course. But it's been more than a week now, and I'm starting to feel free in a strange way. I can start with a clean slate. I still have a lot of questions about myself and the future, but now I can work on them without carrying around the burden of how Dennis is affected by what I do."

A knock on the door startled them both.

"Are you two in there?" their mother asked. "We're ready to turn on the lights on the tree."

Ted popped up and pulled open the door. "Be right down, Mom."

Liz continued down the hall. Ted looked back at Julie. "Coming?"

"In a minute."

Ted left and Julie reached under her pillow. She opened the card and read it again, several times. She had not told her brother the whole story. No one knew the truth about Larry Paxton. Her feelings for him last summer, which were renewed during his October visit, and the new warmth she sensed from him—she was not sure what it all meant, but she needed to find out. If nothing else, she was grateful for his intuitive response to her paintings. But knowing Larry had somehow complicated her feelings about Dennis.

She slipped the card back into the envelope and put it in the drawer of her nightstand. The other two cards still lay on the bed. She would have to open them later.

Julie went downstairs to rejoin the Christmas festivities with her family.

sixteen

Julie woke early on Christmas morning. The sun was just coming up; the house was quiet. Later in the morning Marjorie, Ted, and an assortment of other relatives would descend on the peaceful house. For now, Julie had a chance to sit quietly for a few moments in front of the tree and savor the day.

She slid her feet into slippers and threw a robe around her shoulders and went downstairs. The living room was dim, and she was glad. She wanted to turn on the tree lights and watch them sparkle before daylight filled the room. In the grayness of the early morning, she reached into the corner and plugged in the lights on the official Covington tree.

"Pretty."

Julie jumped at the sound of her grandmother's voice. She stood up and turned around to see Grammy, sitting in an armchair across the room.

"Grammy!" Julie said, surprised. "What are you doing up so early?"

"Li. . .nice."

"Yes, the lights are nice, aren't they?" Julie crossed the room and kissed her grandmother's cheek. "This is like when I was little and you and I would get up early and drink hot chocolate."

Grammy did not respond. Apparently she was through talking. But she looked at the tree with a vague smile on her face. Perhaps she also remembered the early mornings of Julie's childhood. Or perhaps she remembered something else.

❧

Naturally her mother was furious. Julienne had expected nothing less when she broke the news that she had decided to stay in Chicago for the Christmas holidays. She sent a short note, knowing that as soon as her mother received it she would telephone—and she did. Julienne listened calmly but held to her decision.

The difficulty was that she did not dare tell her mother the true reason: she wanted to be with Colin. If her mother knew that, she would jump to all sorts of premature conclusions. The Covingtons and the Leeds were old family friends. If Julienne's mother thought there was the possibility of a romantic relationship between Colin and Julienne, no doubt she would suddenly give her blessing to her daughter's nursing studies in Chicago. Julienne was not sure yet just how she felt about Colin or how he felt about her. But intuition told her that she should not involve her mother, not yet anyway.

Colin had been surprised by her choice to stay in Chicago and at first questioned whether she was certain.

"I hope you haven't made a hasty decision that you'll regret," he had said. And for a moment she had wavered.

Remembering the instant that she had made her choice, she admitted, "Perhaps it was hasty, but I think it's the right one."

He smiled mischievously. "In that case, I'll admit that I like the idea of having someone to spend Christmas with."

That was when she was certain she had chosen well.

The rest of the term had flown by; she had sailed through her exams confidently. And now it was Christmas Eve, and she was standing in church next to Colin, listening to his robust baritone voice carry the melodies of favorite Christmas carols. They had been to church together before and she had heard him sing. But tonight his voice seemed especially full and vibrant, trembling with conviction for the words he sang. She mouthed the words along with the rest of the swollen holiday congregation, but more than once she found herself caught up in listening to Colin.

The hymn ended and they sat down in the crowded pew. Julienne looked around the sanctuary. Signs of the holy season were everywhere—lights, holly, banners, a double choir singing antiphonal anthems. It was an eleven o'clock service that would let out at midnight, a joyous celebration of Christ's birth.

Earlier in the day, Colin and Julienne had taken a small gift to Thomas, who was at last free of his cast. His pleasure at receiving the toy, and the tears that came to his mother's eyes at the thought that anyone would care whether her son had a new toy for Christmas, had nearly overwhelmed Julienne. Giving was such a simple thing but carried so much meaning.

Gradually the lights in the sanctuary were dimmed and candles were passed around. With pebbles of light spattered around the sanctuary, 400 people began singing "Silent Night" in gentle tones. Julienne sang the familiar words quietly, touched by their simple message.

And then the pipe organ swelled and the trumpets joined in. The choir launched into a thunderous rendition of "Joy to the World!" that roused the congregation to their feet. Light burst over the congregation. The coming of Christ was once again announced with great joy.

After the benediction, as the organ moved into a festive postlude, Julienne turned to Colin and sighed with deep satisfaction, "I love Christmas Eve."

"Me, too," he answered. "This is what really matters, isn't it? It gives meaning to everything else we do."

She smiled her agreement.

They heard a cry from the back of the sanctuary. "It's snowing!"

"Perfect!" Julienne nearly squealed with delight.

Once they had exchanged Christmas greetings with the pastor, retrieved their coats from the cloakroom, and bundled up against the cold, they stepped out through the front doorway of the church. Christmas greetings rang in the air up and down the sidewalk as fellow worshipers spoke to each other. Falling snow dusted the heads and shoulders of people as they walked and fragile flakes glistened under the street lamps. The few children who had been permitted to stay up for the midnight service slid along the pavement wishing for new skates for Christmas.

Julienne stuck out her tongue and tried to catch a snowflake. On the fourth attempt she got one and savored the cold tingling on her tongue as it melted instantly.

Colin watched with amusement. "That looks like something Thomas would do."

"Try it! It's fun!"

Her exuberance was contagious, and the usually staid intern turned his face into the snowfall and stuck out his tongue. Laughing, they looked at each other with dancing eyes. Julienne's heart quickened. She was not sure what caused her sudden breathlessness.

Colin reached for her hand. "Come on," he said. "We'll take the long way home."

They turned off the main street that would have taken them directly back to her dormitory in only six blocks. Instead, they took a wide swinging route around the neighborhood, pointing out decorations, admiring trees, humming carols together.

"Maybe we should have gone straight back. Are you sure you won't get in trouble for this?" Colin asked at one point. "Don't you still have a curfew?"

"How can anyone object to my going to church on Christmas Eve?" She stuck out her tongue for another snowflake. It was snowing quite heavily now.

"Church is over, or haven't you noticed." His words were stern but his tone was playful.

"I noticed. Mrs. Davis went to her daughter's house for a couple of days. There are only two of us left in the dorm and she said she trusted us to use good judgment."

Colin tilted his head, as if in thought. "If she saw you now, what would she think about your judgment?"

Julienne swatted his forearm. "Don't persecute me." She tentatively slid one foot along the pavement. "It's getting nice and slippery out here. I haven't been ice skating in ages."

"We'll go soon."

"Really? Can we?"

Colin laughed out loud at her childish excitement and put an arm around her shoulder. "Let's turn here."

She knew he was trying to steer her back to her dorm, and she knew that she should go. It was after one o'clock in the morning. But between the church service and the snow, she was enjoying herself thoroughly and clung to every moment and sensation. Her heart was fuller than it had been for months, maybe even years.

When they arrived back at the dorm, it was dark except for one dim lamp in the lobby. Its glow cast a yellowish tint over the lace tablecloth covering the table on which the lamp sat sat and it beckoned Colin and Julienne to the cozy corner.

"Oops, we're tracking snow," Colin said, stopping abruptly a few steps into the room.

Julienne kicked off her shoes. Self-consciously, Colin did the same, and she set his next to hers beside the door.

"We'd better let these coats dry off," she said, holding her hands out for his overcoat. He obliged, and she draped both coats over hooks next to the door.

Colin seemed a little nervous. "Are you sure it's all right

that I'm here?"

"You've been in the lobby lots of times."

"But not when the place was so deserted. I mean, Mrs. Davis—"

"Is not here." Julienne finished his sentence.

"I don't want to take advantage of her absence."

"It's all right, Colin. It's Christmas!" She gestured that he should sit down. "Do you want some coffee? I could start some."

"Thanks, but don't bother." He was still nervous. He spotted a scraggly, bare, tiny Christmas tree, propped up in one corner. "What's that?"

Julienne blushed. "My feeble attempt at a Christmas tree. I saw it today and it didn't cost much, so I brought it home. Then I realized I don't having anything to put on it or even anything to stand it up in."

"Well, let's see." Colin glanced around the room. "How about a pot from the kitchen?"

"A pot?"

"Yes, get a pot."

When she returned with a dutch oven he stood ready with an afghan to tuck into the pot at the base of the tree. The tree wobbled a little, but it stood.

"There," he said, "now for the decorations." He spied Mrs. Davis's sewing basket. A strand of red ribbon hung over one edge. "Ribbon, of course." He bent down and found the spool. "Looks like there are several yards on here." He threw one end over the top of the tree and began unwinding the spool, walking in circles around the tree as he did.

"Oh, I know," Julienne said, getting into the spirit. "We need some snow on the tree." She scrambled around the room gathering up the small lace doilies that protected the tables from the coffee mugs students often had in the room. Finding seven, she spaced them proportionately around the tree and hung them on the branches.

"It's beautiful," raved Colin, and they collapsed on the couch together, laughing at their creation.

Outside they heard the faint sound of late night carolers singing in the street. In silence they cocked their heads to listen.

" 'O Little Town of Bethlehem,' " Colin announced.

"One of my favorites," Julienne murmured.

They sat quietly and strained to hear. The mood between them had taken a turn toward the somber. When the carolers moved on, the silence between them continued for a moment.

Colin slipped his hand inside his jacket pocket and pulled out a small package. As he did, Julienne's hand went to the package in the pocket of her skirt. She had kept it there all evening, not knowing when the time might come that she could give Colin a gift. They had not discussed exchanging gifts, and she had not been sure what to expect.

"This isn't much, but since you're away from your family I wanted you to have something to open," Colin explained, handing her the package.

Nervously she pulled at the plain red wrapping paper, trying not to tear it. Inside, wrapped in a layer of tissue, was a brooch with a red stone.

"It's very pretty, Colin. Thank you."

He seemed almost apologetic. "It's just costume jewelry, of course, but I hope you like it."

"Oh, yes, I do." She fumbled with the catch and placed the brooch on her shoulder.

"Here, let me help you." At the moment, Colin's big hands were more nimble than her own, and he successfully pinned the brooch in place. As he did so, his knuckles brushed against her chin and their heads were bent close together. Julienne liked the sensation that surged through her.

Flushing slightly, she reached into her pocket for the thin, rectangular box with a simple gold ribbon around it. "This is for you."

Colin pulled the ribbon off and opened the lid. "A new fountain pen." He smiled. "I suppose you've noticed that the one I use all the time is leaking quite badly."

Julienne nodded and smiled. "A doctor ought not to walk around with ink blotches on his fingers."

"It'll remind me of you." He pulled off the cap and examined the point.

"Really?" Instantly she thought that she sounded over eager.

"Whenever I use it." He snapped the cap back on and put the pen safely in his pocket.

"Colin, I. . ." She looked into his gray eyes that seemed to gleam in the softly lit room. "I just want you to know I'm really glad I decided to stay in Chicago for Christmas."

"I am, too. I was jealous that you were going to go home, but mostly I was afraid I would miss you too much."

"Really?" she said again. She knew she sounded like an incredulous child, but she couldn't stop herself.

Colin nodded. "We're friends, right, Julienne?"

"Yes, of course we are." The lump in her throat almost kept her from talking.

"I know you were in love with Lorenzo when we met. . ." He faltered with uncharacteristic insecurity. "But if in time you think that your feelings for me could change, I. . .well, I think we could be more than friends."

Julienne bit on her lower lip and looked down at her lap, her heart pounding. "Lorenzo meant a lot to me," she said quietly. "But he's gone. And he's part of the past."

"It still hurts, doesn't it?"

"I suppose it always will, a little bit. But I have my whole life ahead of me. Maybe I didn't really know what I wanted when I fell in love with Lorenzo." She looked up at him directly. "And it's because of you. You've been a real friend. You've let me discover for myself who I am."

"I only want what's best for you, for you to be everything God means for you to be."

"I know. And when you say that, I really believe it. I'm only now beginning to understand that I can be somebody. I can mean something to other people."

"Like Thomas."

"Yes, and Mary."

"And me."

She felt her jaw dropping, but she did not know what to say.

"I think I love you, Julienne Leed. No, I'm sure I do. I hope that somehow you can grow to love me."

She smiled through the tears in her eyes and nodded. She had never expected him to say what he did. And she had not imagined how glad she would be to hear those words.

"Colin, I do care for you. That's why I stayed in Chicago."

He reached for her hands and held them between his own. They leaned in toward each other, their foreheads touching.

"Merry Christmas, Julienne."

"Merry Christmas, Colin."

Then he kissed her.

seventeen

"What are you doing out here, you crazy kid?" The back door swung open behind Julie, and Ted emerged from the kitchen to sit on the back stoop beside her. He rubbed his palms together against the cold.

"I'm sketching. What does it look like I'm doing?" Julie did not lift her head and her hand never stopped its swift, steady motion with a charcoal pencil. On her left hand she wore a mitten, but the knuckles on her right hand were red from exposure to the cold.

"It's freezing! Can't you sketch out here in the summer like a reasonable human being?"

"Can't do a winter scene in the middle of July."

"Have you heard of a window? It's a modern invention that lets you stay inside and look outside at the same time."

"The lighting is not the same that way."

"You have an answer for everything, don't you?"

"Yep." She kept sketching.

Ted looked over her shoulder at the drawing of their childhood backyard. A rabbit was darting across the yard, kicking up snow dust with its hind legs. Julie had captured its lone crisscross action against a setting of barren, winter-stripped trees and the scraggly branches of the hedge. The layer of snow showed patches of ground in the spots touched by the sun.

"That's pretty good," Ted said quietly. "I can remember sitting out here when I was a little boy watching the rabbits. I never knew where they went in the winter time and I worried about them."

Julie looked at her brother. "Really? I never knew that."

"Little boys were not supposed to tell people they were worried about rabbits," Ted said.

"I never knew you to fit anyone else's idea of what you should be."

"With four sisters around the house, I had to be my own man or I would never have survived."

Julie nudged him with her elbow. "Cut it out. We had nothing to do with it. Who you are is your own fault."

"Well, then, I accept the credit. I like who I am."

Julie resumed her sketching. "That's nice," she muttered.

"Before you tune me out again, I want to know about your hot plans for tonight."

"What hot plans?"

"It's New Year's Eve! Don't tell me you have no plans."

"Sorry to disappoint you, but I don't."

"We'll have to remedy that."

"There's nothing to remedy, Ted. I don't feel much like going out."

"You've spent the entire last week with a sketch pad in one hand and a paint brush in the other. Mom says you've hardly been out of your studio except to eat—and not often enough to suit her."

"It's been a very happy week."

"Right," he said dourly. "I can see the joy shining in your face."

"All right," she admitted, her voice breaking, "so I haven't exactly been on top of the world. I'm not as self-confident as you are."

"Don't start analyzing everything. I just want you to relax and have some fun tonight. My buddy, Jim, is having a party. Nothing too strenuous. Low-key, just games, music, waiting for midnight. Why don't you come?"

She looked at him and smiled. "Am I so pitiful that my brother has to take me to a party?"

"Have you got a better offer?"

"Well. . .no. But I think I'll pass anyway."

Ted sighed, exasperated. He knew it was time to give up. "Don't stay out here too long," he warned as he stood up.

"I'm almost finished."

Inside a few minutes later, Julie sat in the kitchen with her hands cupped around a mug of steaming hot chocolate, grateful for the comfort it gave. Sketching outside in the winter invigorated her, but she had to admit that the fingers on her ungloved hand were almost numb from the cold. I should be more sensible, she chided herself. Then she shook her head to wave away that notion. Being sensible would have meant marrying Dennis, and she couldn't do that.

Her mother came in from the dining room. "Warming up yet?"

Julie smiled. "It is pretty cold out there."

Liz moved to the stove and turned on the fire under the teakettle. "There's a letter for you out in the living room."

"A letter?" Julie perked up.

"Yes. It looks like it's from your friends in Maine."

"I hope Della is not mad at me. I haven't been very good about answering her letters." She slid off her stool. "I'd better go see what it is."

Alone in the living room, she slit the envelope and pulled out the letter. To her surprise, it was in Larry's handwriting. She supposed it was the thank you note for the portrait of his mother, but one glance told her that it was too long for that. Trembling strangely, she began to read.

Dear Julie,

Do you remember that little green book we found in the wall last summer? I'm sure you do, because you spent a lot of time reading it. I don't think Mom ever got around to reading it. She works too hard at everything else around here. But I found it on a shelf in the parlor a couple of weeks ago and opened it up. At first I was reading it on a lark—it's a unique way to get a picture of life so many years ago. Reading about a teenage girl was kind of fun.

I remember that you had discovered that the girl who wrote it was your grandmother. Perhaps meeting her in October is what interested me in reading it. Anyway, I have read the whole thing now, and I think I have a another piece of the puzzle for you.

People don't normally go around talking about their mother's maiden name, and I'm not sure how to say this now. There is no way you could have known that my mother was a Scorzo. Her father was Lorenzo Scorzo, the man in the green book. He operated an import business for many years in a small town in Maine, about a hundred miles from Seabridge. That was one of the reasons we decided to move up here. Mom wanted to come home, even though her family was all gone.

As I told you last summer, I was very young when Grandpa Scorzo died, and my grandmother died years ago, too. All I really have of him is the American version of his name. Reading the diary gave me a picture of the honorable man that he was, though his decision to leave caused your grandmother great pain.

It's a strange twist on a fairy tale, isn't it? If Lorenzo and Julienne had been allowed to be together, you and

*I would be completely different people. My mother re-
members the gentleness of Grandpa Scorzo and the
genuine affection in the family. And I have seen the
great family that came from your grandmother's choice
to marry Colin Covington. Nevertheless, it's fascinating to think what might have been, if things were different all those years ago.*

*I hope this doesn't shock you too much. I'm sorry
there's no way to let your grandmother know whatever became of Lorenzo. But it was a long time ago,
and she was young, so perhaps it wouldn't matter anyway.*

*Why don't you come to Maine and paint? Didn't
you tell me you had the whole month of January off
from school? We got buried in snow over Christmas
and everything is gorgeous. The gallery owner was
impressed with the photos you sent of your paintings.
I'm sure he wants to buy some. If you came to Maine
for a few days, you could negotiate in person. Let me
know what you think.*

> *Warmly,*
> *Larry*

Julie did not know what to think. When Lorenzo left, he
had not gone more than a hundred miles away. Perhaps if her
grandmother had not gone off to nursing school in Chicago,
they would have found each other again when she was a little
older. Would that have changed anything?

Lorenzo Scorzo was Della Paxton's father. Julie was flab-
bergasted to learn that the first man her grandmother had loved
had become Larry's grandfather! It was too incredible to believe. She knew Della was Italian but very little more about
her background. And Larry was a common enough name; it

had never occurred to her that it was a form of Lorenzo.

Her hot chocolate had grown cold. Julie sat and stared at the letter in her lap.

"All you all right, honey?"

She looked up to see her father standing next to her.

"Yes, I think so."

"Are you sure? You look pale." He put his hand against her forehead.

"I feel fine, Dad."

Tom started to walk away, but Julie had an impulse to stop him.

"Dad?"

"Yes?"

"Can I ask you something?"

Tom sat down next to his youngest child on the couch. "What is it, Julie?"

She did not know where to begin. "Something happened last summer that I haven't shared with you and Mom." She saw the alarm in her father's eyes and quickly put him at ease. "Nothing bad, Dad. Everything's fine. But I found something at Leed House in the summer, a book. A diary, actually."

"A diary?"

"Yes. Apparently it had gotten stuck in a wall when the large parlor was divided into two rooms. Larry and Della took the wall out, and we found it."

"Whose was it?"

"It didn't have a name in it. But as I got farther into it, I realized it was Grammy's diary."

Tom's eyes widened. "My mother's?"

"Right. From when she was seventeen years old."

"Wow! I'd like to see that."

"I left it at Leed House. It really belongs to them, and Della wanted to keep it around for guests to look at, since it was written by someone who lived in the house."

Tom pushed out his lower lip thoughtfully. "I have a feeling there's more to your story."

Julie sighed. "There is. Have you ever heard of someone named Lorenzo Scorzo?"

Tom shook his head blankly.

"Grammy wrote about him a lot in her diary," Julie explained. "She was in love with him. Grandpa was a friend of the family and she went out with him because her parents wanted her to. But she was in love with Lorenzo Scorzo. And it turns out he never left Maine. I wonder if Grammy would have ever come to Chicago if she knew he was so close by?"

"She was only seventeen," Tom said, shrugging. "It was young love, a first love."

"But it seemed so sincere in the diary."

"I'm sure it was." Tom smiled and looked at his daughter mischievously. "Don't you remember your first boyfriend. What was his name, the kid with the long hair?"

"Erik." Julie laughed. "I thought he was the true love of my life."

"You were sincere, as I recall."

"I was. . .until I found him holding hands at the mall with Patty Reynolds." Julie saw her father's point but was not quite satisfied. "Daddy, did Grammy love Grandpa?"

"Why do you ask that?" Tom said, surprised.

"The way she wrote about Lorenzo. . .she really cared about him, even if she was just a teenager. I just wonder if she loved Grandpa the same way."

Tom leaned back to answer his daughter's questions. "My father was a gentle man, a patient man. He adored my mother until the moment he died. I can remember watching them sneak kisses when I was a little boy and they didn't think I was watching. And when he died, well, my mother was devastated to say the least." He looked at Julie. "I wish you could have known him."

"Me, too."

"Do you think she felt that way when she married him?"

"We can't really know the truth about that, can we? I'd like to think she married him because she loved him. After he died, she talked for a long time about how she would never have accomplished what she did if he had not believed in her. I think she loved him for that belief."

Julie nodded thoughtfully.

"I have to go see a couple of patients at the hospital," Tom said, squeezing his daughter's knee. "We can talk some more about this later if you want to."

Julie smiled up at him and nodded as he left.

Abandoning her cold chocolate on the coffee table, Julie took the letter and went up to her room and read it several times. About the third time through, she realized that Larry was extending a genuine invitation for her to come to Maine during January. She could, if she wanted to. She had enough credits toward graduation that she did not have to enroll for the intensive winter term during the month of January.

The short day had already grown dark. The long evening stretched before Julie. Ted had already left for his own apartment. Her parents were going out to a party and she would have the house to herself. She would have plenty of time to think.

She wondered what it would be like to be with Della and Larry now that she knew the truth about Lorenzo.

eighteen

The next day was New Year's Day. When Julie got up and went downstairs in search of coffee, her parents were still in bed. The house was still. The new year had snuck in under a cloudy sky.

Ted had tried again last night to get her to go to the party with him, but she had declined once again. She was not in a party mood. If she had gone, more than likely she would have hibernated in a corner and brooded about the news in Larry's letter. Then what would have been the point of being at a party?

Tom and Liz had gone out to a party with church friends. Julie stayed home, watched the television coverage of the ball dropping in Times Square, and went to bed right after midnight. But she had not slept well. Her dreams drifted back seventy-five years to when her grandmother was young with her whole life ahead of her. The girl with the long blond hair stood in front of Leed House with three little brothers scampering around. Suddenly a heavy shadow crossed the girl's face, a forefunner to the dark looming figure that soon dominated the picture. The shadow grew and mutated until Julie could no longer recognize the setting and woke with a sense of horror.

By the time she went downstairs for coffee, Julie had been awake for several hours. She had tried to distract herself with reading or sketching, but her attempts were unsuccessful.

In the kitchen, she fixed a fresh pot of coffee and waited for it to brew. The house was cold; her father had always insisted on turning the thermostat down for the night, even in the dead of winter. The furnace would not kick on again until six o'clock, still twenty minutes away. Julie wrapped her flannel robe more tightly around herself and shivered while standing on the cold tile floor. She should at least have thought to put on some socks before coming downstairs.

The coffeemaker rumbled and the dripping started. Julie turned to watch it, as if doing so would make it happen faster. Other than the background hum of the refrigerator, she heard no other sound.

Staring at the brown liquid pushing through the filter, Julie remembered other quiet mornings. . .from the time before her grandmother was sick. Grammy was an early riser, at least during the part of her life that Julie had known her. As a child, whenever Julie woke up early and no one else in the house was awake, she could telephone her grandmother. No matter how early Julie got up, Grammy was always up earlier, or so it had seemed to Julie. They would sit on stools in two separate kitchens and have a long talk about their dreams and what they meant. When Julie got to be a teenager, she started sleeping later; it seemed to be the adolescent thing to do. And the early morning phone calls with her grandmother had stopped.

Julie missed those talks, now more than ever.

The coffee was finished brewing. She filled a mug, cradled it in both hands, and started back up the stairs to get something on her feet. As she passed the room that her grandmother had been in for two years, Julie stopped. The room was much as Grammy had left it. It had too much furniture in it, because Grammy had insisted on having some of her own things around when she moved in with her son. The tops of the dresser and end tables were heaped with memorabilia, old photos, trinkets, and many other items that no one besides her grandmother knew the significance of. Grammy was not allowed to take much with her to the nursing home, so they had only packed her clothes and a few photos that had hung on the wall in her room at home.

Julie decided to go in. She had a sudden urge to dig out an old scrapbook she used to see her grandmother with a lot. It was red, she remembered, and some of the pages were loose. She took a gulp of her coffee and set the mug down on a pile of old magazines. The bottom of the nightstand had a storage area behind a small door. She opened it and riffled through the papers in there. No photo albums or scrapbooks. Next she ran her hands along the bookshelves, filled with odds and ends, souvenirs of vacations, boxes of old letters. She stopped in the middle of the second shelf, her fingers resting on a tattered green box. Julie could remember seeing her grandmother sitting with that box years and years ago. Why hadn't she ever noticed it on the shelf before this?

Carefully, she pried it out from the bottom of the pile and held it in both hands. Backing up slowly to sit on the end of the bed, she lifted the torn lid. She felt a twinge of guilt as she did so; she was invading her grandmother's privacy. But her curiosity overwhelmed her. She tucked her still cold feet under the edge of her bathrobe and set the lid aside. A dozen letters were tied with a ribbon; an envelope held an assortment of old photographs, faded with age.

Julie's heart pounded as she contemplated reading the letters. They might answer some of her questions. She reasoned that if her grandmother could communicate, she would gladly answer Julie's questions. Julie set the box down and held the packet of letters in her hands. Slowly she pulled one end of the ribbon and the knot came free. The paper crinkled as she unfolded the first letter. She did not recognize the handwriting.

My dear Julienne,

I am dismayed that we have to be apart so soon after our wedding. But this training in New York is for only six weeks, and then we can be together again, and I do not intend to leave you for a long, long time.

Sometimes I can hardly believe that you married me. How lucky I am to have you! What a beautiful gift from God, more than I ever asked Him for. I thank Him each day that He taught your heart to love Him and to love me.

Write to me every day, won't you? I am working long, hard hours here, and the refreshment that a letter from you brings is beyond description.

Yours always,
Colin

Julie was reading a love letter from the grandfather she had never known. And some of her questions were being answered. She unfolded the next letter and checked the date. It was just a few days after the first one. Quickly she flipped through the whole stack. He had written his bride twice a week for the whole six weeks that they were separated. Julie read every letter, being careful to refold each one when she was finished.

A portrait of Colin Covington emerged: a man of dedication to his work, adoration for his wife, obedience to God's direction. When she imagined her grandfather, Julie always thought of him as old. But in these letters he was a young man, a newlywed, an intern pediatrician embarking on a medical career in the poor neighborhoods of Chicago.

Julie picked up the box and dumped the photos on the bed. Youthful images of her grandmother stared up at her, the face in the pictures not so different from her own. And there were pictures of her grandfather, too. . .pictures she had never seen before, from the early years of their marriage. Their brown hues had faded with time and the corners were crinkled, but their significance endured.

At first Julie thought the wad of yellowed tissue was trash that should have been discarded decades ago. But when she picked it up and felt its weight in her fist, she knew it held one of Grammy's secret treasures. Carefully she unfolded the crackling paper and exposed the contents: a costume jewelry brooch with a ruby red stone. Julie turned it over, hoping for an inscription. Instead she saw only a broken clasp. Obviously the piece had no money value; but it must have been priceless to her grandmother. Julie only wished she could know why.

Julie opened the last letter.

> *Dear Julienne,*
>
> *I may see you before this letter reaches you, but I will write anyway. I miss you terribly but writing to you like this makes me feel as if we are together for a few minutes. I only wish I could have written more during the last few weeks.*
>
> *A colleague here has offered me a job. He has been in New York for several years now and wants to go back to Chicago. His dream is to open a clinic specializing in caring for children. He wants me to be his partner. It will mean long hours with just the two of us to share them, and I don't suppose it will pay much. I'm sure we could find room on the staff for a good nurse, if you're interested.*
>
> *When I get home we can talk about the details and make a final decision. I feel, though, that perhaps this is the opportunity God has been preparing me for, the reason why He has given me such a yearning to work*

with children. I have been praying steadily for two weeks. I am eager now to hear your counsel, since this decision will affect the direction of our life together.

The sites of New York and the fascinating procedures I have learned here pale against the thought of you, the sound of your voice, the softness of your skin, and the prospect of being with you again soon.

Love,
Colin

Julie had a lump in her throat. She had known that her grandfather had started out in a small pediatric partnership in Chicago. But he had eventually moved out to the burgeoning suburbs and the details of those early years had been lost. Time had pulsed forward into the second and third generations of Covingtons in Illinois, and the dreams of two young people from New England were reduced to the contents of a torn, green cardboard box.

As she folded up the last letter and replaced everything in the box, Julie heard her parents moving around in the hallway. She glanced at her watch. She had been sitting and going through her grandmother's things for nearly two hours.

Suddenly she decided what she wanted to do with her free day. Painting could wait. Julie showered and dressed quickly. She patted her shirt pocket to make sure the brooch was safe there. She wanted to be ready to go as soon as possible.

A few minutes later she whizzed into the kitchen and caught her mother toasting english muffins.

"Shall I put one in for you?" Liz asked.

"No, thanks, Mom. I don't have time." Julie opened the fridge and pulled out the orange juice. She reached into the cupboard for a glass.

"Where are you off to in such a hurry?"

Julie swallowed her orange juice nearly in one gulp. "I'm going to see Grammy."

"It's only nine o'clock in the morning, Julie. She might not even be awake yet."

"Doesn't matter." Julie set her glass in the sink and started stuffing her arms into her jacket. "I want to see her."

She was out the door before her mother could say another word.

nineteen

Julie pulled into a parking spot right outside the front door of Prairie Village Nursing Center. Apparently New Year's morning was not a popular time for visitors; the few other cars in the lot all bore employee stickers. She glanced at her watch: 9:17. Mentally she scanned the printed schedule she had once seen of Prairie Village's daily routine. Grammy should be either in her own room or the day room off the cafeteria.

Pulling open the heavy door, Julie stepped into the lobby and went to the desk to sign in. She did not recognize the nursing assistant behind the desk, who was bleary eyed and had obviously been to a late party. More amused than sympathetic, Julie thought about greeting her cheerily, but decided not to. She simply signed her name in the guest book and went looking for her grandmother.

She opted to check out the day room first. There were half a dozen residents in wheelchairs scattered around the large room and a dozen others sitting on the couches or at the game tables. Some were working on puzzles, others were reading, others just sitting. Julie scanned the group.

"Well, look who's here."

Julie turned her head and settled her eyes on Isabel Jackson, her grandmother's roommate.

"Hello, Mrs. Jackson." Julie walked to where Isabel was sitting with Grammy on a small sofa. She knelt and took her grandmother's hands. "Happy New Year, Grammy."

"Happy," Grammy said.

"You look good."

Grammy smiled, seeming to understand. Julie was momentarily encouraged.

"How's your young man?" Isabel barked.

A bit flustered by the question, Julie fumbled for an answer. "Well. . .we. . .um. . . ." How could she explain what had happened between her and Dennis? Still holding Grammy's hand, she stood up.

"He was sure nice, that fellow from Maine."

Julie swallowed. Isabel was talking about Larry, not Dennis.

"Yes, he is," Julie said weakly.

"When are you going to see him again?"

"I'm not sure."

"He sure is carrying the torch for you."

Julie's eyes widened slightly. Whatever made Isabel Jackson think such a thing?

"He's a friend that I met last summer," Julie said. "We don't really know each other very well."

"Don't have to know somebody very well to carry a torch."

Julie blushed. "Really, I don't think—"

Isabel waved away her protests. "You'll figure it out sooner or later." She glanced at Julienne. "Your grandmother's been quite the chatterbox lately."

"Really?" Julie, her face flushed, was glad for the change in subject.

"Don't know what pushed her button, but she goes on and on all day long."

Julie was puzzled. Her grandmother had spoken less and less over the last few months. "What does she talk about?"

"Long ago stuff, mostly, but clear as a bell."

"Long ago?"

"Was your grandfather's name Colin?"

Julie nodded.

"She carries on about him all the time. And some little boy named Thomas."

"My father?"

"No, someone else. Before she was married. Fell from a window."

"Oh. I don't know who that would be."

"She seems quite fond of him."

Julie shrugged one shoulder. "Must be someone she knew. It's not one of her brothers."

"Must have named your dad after him."

"You think so?"

"That's my judgment."

"Perhaps you're right. I never heard if there was a special reason for Dad's name." Julie looked at the two old women sitting side by side so companionably. "Thank you for sitting with her like you do."

"My pleasure. I like the company."

Julie smiled, still amused by the thought that anyone would think of Grammy as real company. She was grateful for Isabel and her odd ways.

"Maybe she'd like to go for a walk," Julie suggested.

"Sure. Beat the crowd. Take her for a few laps. She needs the exercise."

Julie laughed. "Right. Come on, Grammy. Let's go down to the end of the hall." She turned to Isabel. "Do you want to come?"

"I can do my own laps," Isabel said. "You kids go on."

Julie helped her grandmother to her feet and positioned herself beside her with an arm around her waist. Grammy had never fallen, but she shuffled in such a slow, fragile manner that Julie was always afraid that she would fall, and she could not help offering extra protection with her arm.

"I like Isabel, don't you?" Julie said softly as they inched down the hall.

"Like, yes. Bel."

"You're lucky to have made a friend so quickly here."

Grammy's gaze still focused on the floor ahead of her, but she seemed to smile slightly.

Julie continued to murmur a running commentary on objects in the hallway, from drooping Christmas decorations to worn out carpeting and plastic plants. Occasionally her grandmother echoed back a phrase.

"Did you like your Christmas presents?" Julie asked. Grammy had received a couple of new sweaters, a pair of slippers, and a handmade lap quilt.

"Pin."

"Pin?" Julie asked. No one had given a Grammy a pin.

"Pin nice."

"Did someone here give you a pin for Christmas?" Perhaps Isabel had offered something on the holiday.

"Col. Col."

"Colin?"

Grammy smiled.

She's thinking of years ago, Julie surmised. She touched the small lump in her shirt pocket. Was the red brooch the special pin Grammy was thinking of?

Julie steered her grandmother toward a bench in the hall. "Here, Grammy, let's sit for a moment. I have something to show you."

When they were settled, Julie reached into her pocket for the wad of tissue. As she unwrapped it, she glanced at Grammy, who was staring in the other direction.

She gently took her grandmother's chin with one hand. "Look here, Grammy. Can you see this?"

Grammy lowered her eyes and focused on the brooch. "Pin."

"Yes," Julie said, encouraged by the response so far.

"Pin." Grammy took hold of the brooch and closed her fist over it tightly.

"Do you want to keep the pin, Grammy? We could put it in your room."

Her grandmother's response was to clench the pin even more tightly.

"Good. You keep it." Julie stood up and offered a hand to her grandmother. "Let's go back and find Isabel."

They started back down the hall. While she continued to make one-sided small talk, Julie contemplated the possibility of trying to tell her grandmother about Larry and Della's relationship to Lorenzo. But would Grammy even remember meeting Larry? It had been almost three months since his visit. And even if she were in perfect health, would she be interested in news about what had become of Lorenzo?

With a flash, Julie remembered that when Larry had visited, Grammy had said Lor. Had she seen something of Lorenzo in his grandson? Or was it just a nonsense syllable with no significance, like many of the other sounds that came from Grammy? Or maybe a lot of those sounds did mean something, but no one knew quite what.

Julie looked at her grandmother tenderly and sighed. How she wished she could be sure that Grammy could understand. Then she might try to tell her what she had discovered, to share secrets like they had when Julie was little. There were moments when it seemed like she understood, or when she made eye contact for a fraction of a second. But was that enough? Julie thought not. She decided not to attempt the discussion. She looked again at her grandmother's face and knew there was no need to talk about Lorenzo.

They walked back to the day room. Grammy seemed tired as Julie settled her into a chair. Isabel looked up from the puzzle she was working on.

"She looks worn out."

"Yes, she does," Julie agreed. "I shouldn't push her that way."

"It's good for her heart."

Impulsively Julie decided to ask Isabel a question.

"When she talks about the past, does she ever mention some-one named Lorenzo?"

"Lorenzo? No. Don't think I've heard that from her. Why?"

"No reason, really. It's just someone she used to know. I thought maybe she had mentioned him."

"Sounds foreign."

"He was," Julie said, not knowing why that should matter.

"She just talks about your grandpa."

Julie nodded. "Well, that's good. I'm glad she's saying something." She was satisfied with her choice not to discuss Lorenzo. Perhaps her father had been right: Lorenzo was simply the first love of a teenage girl. Obviously Julienne had built a life with Colin Covington, a life that she treasured more than any memory of Lorenzo.

"Lunch time."

"Huh?" Julie looked up at Isabel.

"It's almost lunch time. Gotta get her down there early."

Julie looked at her watch and saw that she had been at Prairie Valley for nearly two hours. It was indeed time for lunch.

❧

The sun was high and strong, throwing a glare off the blanket of white still on the ground from the Christmas snow. Julie wished she had remembered her sunglasses as she adjusted the visor and squinted out the windshield. The light seemed to distort the images along the roadside and made it difficult for her eyes to focus. She was tempted to stop and sketch, but her hand was still chapped from the day before. Besides, the scene needed some color. It would not work with just a pencil.

Julie tried to distract herself by looking around and planning how she would paint the changing scenery, thinking that perhaps she could come out along the roadway during her free weeks and make some preliminary sketches. But the tactic did not work. Isabel's innocent and friendly inquiry about Larry rang in her ears and the statement that Larry carried a torch for her left her rattled. Did the old woman, who did not hesitate to speak her mind, see something that Julie did not see? What if she were right?

She shook her head as she turned onto the highway that would take her back to Lovellton. Isabel could not possibly be right. Larry had stated his position quite clearly last summer: he liked Julie but did not want her to misinterpret his friendship. She had been careful to guard her feelings after that, especially during his visit in October.

But there was that kiss at the train station. It was only a kiss on the cheek, but his was more than she had ever expected. And his notes lately sounded different somehow, with a warmer, more personal tone. He had gone to so much trouble to show her paintings to the gallery owner in Maine. She hoped she was not misinterpreting again. She could go out to Maine in January with the wrong expectations and make a complete fool of herself, and she did not want to do that. Or she could stay home and wonder about things from a distance and never really know the truth. Hopefully she would find some middle ground, a place that would allow her to discover some answers or at least to be able to verbalize the questions of her heart.

Finding out that Larry was Lorenzo's grandson had only increased her fascination with him. She found herself remembering some of the descriptions in Grammy's diary that she had read in the summer and suddenly seeing similarities in

Larry. Rationally she knew she was making too much of it all, but emotionally she could not stop herself. It was as if somehow knowing Larry better would help her understand her grandmother better. It made no sense, but the urge persisted. She would never be able to squelch it without going to Maine.

Julie sadly thought of Dennis. She should never have dragged her feet with him. Instead of facing her feelings squarely in the fall, she had tried to come home from Maine at summer's end and enjoy a relationship that made sense. In the end, that was not enough, and she was sorry to have hurt him. But his departure also relieved her of some of the guilt she felt in the summer about her interest in Larry. Now she was free to resolve those feelings once and for all, one way or the other.

Home once again, she pulled up into the driveway and parked behind her mother's car. It looked like her parents were both home, spending the day quietly, although Marjorie was due to come over with her family for dinner.

The kitchen was quiet when Julie slipped through the back doorway. She could not point to the exact moment she had made her decision, but she had made one. Without even stopping to remove her jacket, she reached for the phone and quickly dialed.

"Leed House," a cheery voice said after the third ring.

"Hi, Della." Julie had felt a little nervous about Larry possibly answering the phone, so she was relieved when his mother greeted her.

"Julie? Is that really you?"

"Really is. Sorry about not answering your letters. I got bogged down in term papers."

"No need to apologize. You are a student and an artist, not a scribe."

It was good to hear Della's voice. Della Paxton had been a true friend to Julie during her ten weeks in Seabridge, Maine, taking her under her wing, allowing her to paint on the property as much as she liked, offering encouragement and confidential conversation. Julie missed her deeply.

"Larry tells me he's trying to talk you into a visit," Della said. "Is that true?"

"He's mentioned it a couple of times. Actually that's why I'm calling."

"You're coming?"

"I'm sure going to try."

"How long can you stay?"

"About a week, maybe ten days."

"That won't be nearly enough, you know."

Julie smiled and agreed. "Afraid that's the best I can do. Then it's back to the grind."

"Larry will be delighted."

Julie's blood raced momentarily and she pictured his reaction. She hoped Della was right. She forced herself to get back to business.

"Larry thought I should meet with his art gallery friend in person. Maybe you could ask him to try to set up a meeting. I could probably bring a few of the smaller paintings with me."

"I would love to see them myself. I may be the first customer in the gallery if he carries your work."

Julie felt herself blushing, even though Della could not see her. "You've only seen a few things," she said. "A lot of what I've done is pretty average."

"That's not what Larry says."

"Well, anyway," Julie said, redirecting the subject of the conversation, "I think I could be there in about a week, if that would work out for you."

"Of course it would. We'll put you in the room on the second floor that we cleaned up last summer."

"Great. Then I'll see you both a week from today."

She hung up and turned to face her mother coming through the doorway from the dining room.

"See who, honey?" her mother asked lightly. "Are you getting together with some friends during your break?"

Julie took a deep breath. There was no time to waste. She would have to break the news to her family right away.

twenty

The next five days were a whirlwind. Julie had procrasti-
nated about getting her car serviced and had to do that before
she dared drive it to Maine. Ted had teased her mercilessly
about her negligence and having to face the consequences,
and she winced as she wrote the check to pay the mechanic.

She spent one whole day in her makeshift studio taking
photographs of paintings. A few weeks earlier she had sent a
few photos to Maine, but she wanted to go with a complete
portfolio this time. She selected about a dozen to have en-
larged at a professional photo lab, wincing again as she paid
a premium price for same day service. Then it took another
day to arrange the photos and sketches into organized albums
that would display her work. When she was finished, she
stayed up late into the night flipping the pages, sometimes
questioning her choices. Overall she was pleased with the
appearance of the albums. It was her first step toward developing a professional portfolio. She looked around her studio,
which somehow seemed less like just a room off the garage
now that she was taking this step.

Her father had insisted that she meet with his lawyer
before she made any agreements with the owner of the art
gallery. She tried to weasel out of it, but Ted, an attorney
himself, escorted her personally to one of his colleagues who
did a lot of contract work. On the one hand, it scared her.
Legal language mystified her and therefore intimidated her.
Even the office was formal and overbearing; she felt out of
place and tongue-tied. On the other hand, she was thankful

for her father's perseverence. Surprised that anyone was interested in her art at all, she was naive and idealistic enough to agree to anything out of gratitude for the recognition. And her father's insistence meant that he believed that something important might come out of the contact with the gallery owner.

Julie also squeezed in another visit to Grammy, since it would be several weeks before she saw her again. She did not sleep much during the entire five days, but she was too excited to feel fatigued. Questions that had plagued her for years might be answered in the next few days. Could she be an artist? Could she find someone waiting for her who believed in her? She was not sure what she was more nervous about, meeting the gallery owner or seeing Larry again.

On the morning of her scheduled departure, Julie was still packing. She would be gone for only a couple of weeks, but winter clothing was bulky. It was not as simple as throwing shorts and tee shirts into a bag like she had last summer. She knew she was probably packing too much, but she wanted to be sure she would be prepared for a variety of settings. What if the art gallery was an upscale place? She could not show up there in jeans and a sweatshirt, looking like the inexperienced college student she was. First impressions were important. She agonized whether she should take the two wool suits she had inherited from her sister, or whether she should go for the dressy but casual look. In the end she opted for nice sweaters that she could wear with skirts or slacks. And she hoped to enjoy the outdoors while in Maine, maybe even ski, so she needed plenty of warm, protective clothing, too. She was definitely going to need two suitcases.

With clothing neatly folded on her bed, she rummaged in the back of her closet and pulled out a second suitcase. Just as she opened it up, Marjorie entered her room.

"I thought you were supposed to leave first thing this

morning," Marjorie said.

"Well, I didn't quite make it." Julie laid her two newest sweaters in the open suitcase.

"Are you about done?" Marjorie handed her two pair of jeans, freshly laundered.

"Just about." She tucked the jeans in next to the sweaters.

"You know, Seabridge might not be the same as you remember it."

"I was there five months ago. It can't have changed much."

"I don't mean the physical town. That's been there two hundred years. But I hope you're not idealizing a place where you can go when you want to run away from your problems."

Julie whirled around and stared at her sister. "What is that supposed to mean?"

Marjorie started straightening clothes Julie had already packed. "I'm just being realistic. You went to Maine in the summer because you wanted to get away from all the family problems. . .and Dennis, though I'll never understand why you let him walk away. Now you're doing it again."

Julie stopped her sister's repacking efforts. "I can do my own packing, thanks. Marjorie, I am not running away from anything. Haven't you been paying attention at all? There is an art dealer interested in my work. You're always lecturing me about marketability, and now that I have a chance, you find some other reason to criticize me."

"I'm just saying that the timing of this opportunity is very convenient. You break up with Dennis last month and now you take off for Maine."

"The two things have nothing to do with each other." Julie slammed the suitcase shut, even though she was not finished filling it. "And I am not 'taking off' for Maine. I have been invited."

"By someone you barely know. Don't get your hopes up."

Julie swallowed and worked hard to hold on to her temper. "Marjorie, if you are happy with your life, then I'm happy for you. But I would like to live mine."

The bedroom door opened. "What is going on in here?" Liz Covington demanded.

Julie and Marjorie looked at each other sheepishly. No matter how old they got, they could not stop squabbling.

"When are you two going to learn to get along like sensible adults?" Liz asked, with an edge to her voice. "You shouldn't need your mother to break up your fights at your ages."

"Sorry, Mother," Marjorie said. She stepped over and gave Julie a quick kiss on the cheek. "I have to go. The girls are waiting. Have a nice trip."

Marjorie left without any further ruckus. Julie sank onto the bed, her head in one hand.

"I'm sorry, Mom. I always promise myself that I'm not going to let her get to me, but she always does."

"She means well."

"I know," Julie muttered. "You tell me that all the time. But she always finds something to pick on. Now she thinks I'm running away from my problems."

Liz, with a sweatshirt in her hands, sat on the bed, beside her daughter. "Julie, honey, I have to admit that when you left last summer, I didn't understand why. And selfishly I had looked forward to having you around the house."

"That wasn't selfish, Mom. Grammy was a lot of work for you. I just felt so mixed up about things, I had to get away. I was the one being selfish."

Liz shook her head. "It's all right. I'm not blaming you for anything. I just want you to know that this time I understand why you need to go, and I don't mean just because of the art gallery."

Julie looked at her mother, surprised.

Liz continued. "We all liked Dennis, but I've sensed for a long time that you wouldn't marry him."

"How could you tell? I didn't even know myself."

"That doesn't matter. What matters now is that you move forward. If Dennis is not what God has for your future, you need to find out what He does have planned."

"I feel so unsure of myself. I don't know what I feel most of the time."

Liz patted Julie's hand. "That's why you need to go. Don't pay any attention to Marjorie. Your father and I think you should go."

Julie reached out to give her mother a hug. "Thanks, Mom."

"Oh, Julie!" Her father's singsong voice floated up the stairwell and through the open door. "If you're planning to get any farther than the Indiana border today, you'd better get moving." She heard his muffled steps in the carpeted hall, and soon he appeared in her doorway.

"I know, Dad. I'm just about done here." She snapped open the suitcase she had shut angrily a few minutes earlier and dropped in a makeup bag and a couple of necklaces. Before she could get the suitcase latched again, her father whisked it away.

"Come on," he said. "Ted has everything else loaded."

"I hope he was careful with the canvases."

"Of course he was. You can see for yourself."

Julie followed her parents down the stairs, through the house, and into the kitchen. She grabbed her jacket off the hook near the door and then gasped. "A dress coat. I should take a dress coat. Mom, I don't have a decent coat," she pleaded.

Liz smiled obligingly. "You can take my black wool. I can get along without it for a couple of weeks. Take the white scarf, too."

"Thanks, Mom." Julie went to the hall closet, fetched the coat, and returned to the kitchen.

Ted rattled the back door from the outside. "Are you coming or aren't you? It's freezing out here."

"Yes, yes, I'm coming." She stood on tiptoe to kiss her father's cheek and then her mother's. "See you in two weeks."

Ted held the door open and she ventured out into the frigid January air. He followed her to her car, parked at the end of the driveway.

"Well, kiddo, looks like you're going to make a mark for yourself after all."

"Let's not jump to conclusions." Julie could see her warm breath hanging in the air.

"Let's hear some confidence. This is a great opportunity for you."

Secretly Julie wondered if Ted meant meeting with the gallery owner or the chance to see Larry again. Both were important to her.

"I'll give it my best shot," she said, thinking of both challenges.

Ted closed the door behind her and pressed his face up against it, squashing his nose in the frost. Julie laughed and started the engine.

She drove leisurely through the side streets that would take her to the interstate highway. Lovellton had played out its burst of holiday festivities and had returned to the quiet community that it really was. The children had returned to school. Life was back to normal.

But not for Julie. She would have ten days in Seabridge. Would it be enough to answer her questions? Perhaps not, but it was a beginning. She did not know what normal would be from now on. As she accelerated onto the entrance ramp, Julie breathed a sigh of excitement for the path she had chosen.

A Letter To Our Readers

Dear Reader:

In order that we might better contribute to your reading enjoyment, we would appreciate your taking a few minutes to respond to the following questions. When completed, please return to the following:

Rebecca Germany, Editor
Heartsong Presents
P.O. Box 719
Uhrichsville, Ohio 44683

1. Did you enjoy reading *Farther Along the Road*?
   ❑ Very much. I would like to see more books
      by this author!
   ❑ Moderately
      I would have enjoyed it more if _____

   _____

2. Are you a member of *Heartsong Presents*? Yes   No
   If no, where did you purchase this book? _____

   _____

3. What influenced your decision to purchase this
   book? (Check those that apply.)

   ❑ Cover   ❑ Back cover copy

   ❑ Title   ❑ Friends

   ❑ Publicity   ❑ Other _____

4. On a scale from 1 (poor) to 10 (superior), please rate
   the following elements.

   ___Heroine   ___Plot

   ___Hero   ___Inspirational theme

   ___Setting   ___Secondary characters

5. What settings would you like to see covered in
   Heartsong Presents books?

   _____

   _____

6. What are some inspirational themes you would like
   to see treated in future books?_____

   _____

   _____

7. Would you be interested in reading other *Heartsong
   Presents* titles?   ❏ Yes   ❏ No

8. Please check your age range:
   ❏ Under 18   ❏ 18-24   ❏ 25-34
   ❏ 35-45   ❏ 46-55   ❏ Over 55

9. How many hours per week do you read? _____

Name _____

Occupation _____

Address _____

City _____ State _____ Zip _____

MONTANA

Rocky Bluff Chronicles

__*Autumn Love*—A bizarre incident at Rocky Bluff High School literally triggers Edith Harkness's retirement as a home economics teacher, and the start of her so-called golden years. Then Edith meets Roy Dutton, and the last thing she ever expected happens to her. HP66 $2.95

__*Contagious Love*—Despite the promise of Edith's joyous second marriage to Roy Dutton in the autumn of her life, life in this Montana hamlet is anything but blissful. Edith is drawn into a maelstrom of emotions and needs. Never before have her unwavering faith and contagious love been in such demand. HP89 $2.95

__*Inspired Love*—Beth Slater, a single parent of a four-year-old son, has a dream to cling to and the means to acheive it. That is, until now. For Beth to survive, she needs first to claim an inspired love—the love of her Heavenly Father—and then the love of a godly man. HP109 $2.95

__*Distant Love*—Book four in the series coming soon!

...Hearts ♥ng.....

Any 12 *Heartsong Presents* titles for only $26.95 *

CONTEMPORARY ROMANCE IS CHEAPER BY THE DOZEN!

Buy any assortment of twelve *Heartsong Presents* titles and save 25% off of the already discounted price of $2.95 each!

*plus $1.00 shipping and handling per order and sales tax where applicable.

HEARTSONG PRESENTS TITLES AVAILABLE NOW:

__HP 3 RESTORE THE JOY, *Sara Mitchell*
__HP 5 THIS TREMBLING CUP, *Marlene Chase*
__HP 6 THE OTHER SIDE OF SILENCE, *Marlene Chase*
__HP 9 HEARTSTRINGS, *Irene B. Brand*
__HP 10 SONG OF LAUGHTER, *Lauraine Snelling*
__HP 13 PASSAGE OF THE HEART, *Kjersti Hoff Baez*
__HP 14 A MATTER OF CHOICE, *Susannah Hayden*
__HP 21 GENTLE PERSUASION, *Veda Boyd Jones*
__HP 22 INDY GIRL, *Brenda Bancroft*
__HP 25 REBAR, *Mary Carpenter Reid*
__HP 26 MOUNTAIN HOUSE, *Mary Louise Colln*
__HP 29 FROM THE HEART, *Sara Mitchell*
__HP 30 A LOVE MEANT TO BE, *Brenda Bancroft*
__HP 33 SWEET SHELTER, *VeraLee Wiggins*
__HP 34 UNDER A TEXAS SKY, *Veda Boyd Jones*
__HP 37 DRUMS OF SHELOMOH, *Yvonne Lehman*
__HP 38 A PLACE TO CALL HOME, *Eileen M. Berger*
__HP 41 FIELDS OF SWEET CONTENT, *Norma Jean Lutz*
__HP 42 SEARCH FOR TOMORROW, *Mary Hawkins*
__HP 45 DESIGN FOR LOVE, *Janet Gortsema*
__HP 46 THE GOVERNOR'S DAUGHTER, *Veda Boyd Jones*
__HP 49 YESTERDAY'S TOMORROWS, *Linda Herring*
__HP 50 DANCE IN THE DISTANCE, *Kjersti Hoff Baez*
__HP 53 MIDNIGHT MUSIC, *Janelle Burnham*
__HP 54 HOME TO HER HEART, *Lena Nelson Dooley*
__HP 57 LOVE'S SILKEN MELODY, *Norma Jean Lutz*
__HP 58 FREE TO LOVE, *Doris English*
__HP 61 PICTURE PERFECT, *Susan Kirby*
__HP 62 A REAL AND PRECIOUS THING, *Brenda Bancroft*
__HP 65 ANGEL FACE, *Frances Carfi Matranga*
__HP 66 AUTUMN LOVE, *Ann Bell*
__HP 69 BETWEEN LOVE AND LOYALTY, *Susannah Hayden*
__HP 70 A NEW SONG, *Kathleen Yapp*

(If ordering from this page, please remember to include it with the order form.)

····· Presents ·····

Great Inspirational Romance at a Great Price!

Heartsong Presents books are inspirational romances in contemporary and historical settings, designed to give you an enjoyable, spirit-lifting reading experience. You can choose from 120 wonderfully written titles from some of today's best authors like Colleen L. Reece, Brenda Bancroft, Janelle Jamison, and many others.

When ordering quantities less than twelve, above titles are $2.95 each.